Thorhilde

Thorhilde

The Viking Queen

Ole-Bjorn Tobiassen

authorHOUSE®

AuthorHouse™
1663 Liberty Drive
Bloomington, IN 47403
www.authorhouse.com
Phone: 1 (800) 839-8640

Published by AuthorHouse 03/06/2015

ISBN: 978-1-4969-7272-9 (sc)
ISBN: 978-1-4969-7271-2 (hc)
ISBN: 978-1-4969-7270-5 (e)

Library of Congress Control Number: 2015903253

Print information available on the last page.

Any people depicted in stock imagery provided by Thinkstock are models, and such images are being used for illustrative purposes only. Certain stock imagery © Thinkstock.

This book is printed on acid-free paper.

Table of Contents and Chronological Timeline

I dedicate this book to my wife Tove and thank her
for all her support throughout the years. Without
her this book would never have been printed.
Also thanks to our sons Terje Henning and Per
Erik for their drawings to this book
And also thanks to our friends Sandy Albright, Donald and Karen
Quass for kindly having proofread and edited the manuscript.

Chapter I

The Northwestern Settlement-1308

Thorhilde and her grandmother, Gyda, are sitting quietly in their home listening to the summer storm that has suddenly erupted. They listen in awe to the rolling thunder and admire the blitzing lightening that flares over the sky.

"Now, Thor is again riding across the sky in his chariot pulled by two large rams" Gyda says to Thorhilde.

"Is it really so, grandmother?" Thorhilde questions.

Gyda answers "Yes, my girl, he hits the clouds with his hammer and that makes this terrible sound."

"It is frightening!" the little girl blurted out! "Are we in any danger?"

"No, we are not. As baptized Christians, we are protected against evil."

"Grandmother, I remember that you told me once that Thor is one of our ancestors. But, why is he doing all these scary things to us?"

"Thor is probably angry because he was not chosen to lead the Caucasian tribes from their ancestral home in Caucasus toward the Nordic countries. Instead, his father, Odin, chose his younger brother, Viking, for this task."

"Why did our ancestor, Odin, choose Viking instead of Thor?" Thorhilde asked, in surprise.

"Thor was not able to control his temper and he was not a good mediator to all the different clan chiefs they had to negotiate with."

"I feel sorry for him, grandmother, don't you as well? Having to travel the sky forever and take out his frustration in such a way. He is also scaring a lot of people and innocent animals as well."

Gyda looks at her twelve year old granddaughter with love in her eyes. "It is sweet of you, Thorhilde, to have compassion for people, but Thor has really taken this upon himself to become like this."

Thorhilde was just twelve years old and already a stunning beauty. She was of middle height and walked very gracefully. She was often admired by many of the young men. Her hair was slight red blonde and her grandmother told her that she had inherited it either from her Irish or her Scythian ancestors. Most beautiful were her eyes. They were large, blue and glistering like jewels when she was happy, but dark and like daggers when she was angry. She was sometimes very tempermental, but was learning to control it from her grandmother.

Gyda was little and thin. She was gray-haired, with a face that portrayed willpower, integrity and labor. Her eyes were greyish blue and portrayed love and compassion and longings. She had been a widow for many years and was now so worn out that she had some difficulty sometimes in standing up straight for a long time.

"Please tell me about our ancestral home in the Caucasus, grandmother."

"We are descended from one of the lost tribes of Israel, which the Assyrians led north to the Caucasian mountains. We are of the blood of Ephraim and many of us settled later on in Norway, while many of the tribe of Dan settled in Denmark and gave name to that country."

"Grandma, I am listening! Tell me everything that you know of their travels!"

"Well, then I have to begin from the beginning.

"After the disobedient tribes of Northern Israel had been subdued and humiliated by the Assyrians for a thousand years, a very cruel warrior, called Attila, arrived from further east and destroyed the peace that our ancestors had negotiated with the people of the plain, the Scythians."

"Who were the Scythians?" Thorhilde asked in wonder.

"The Scythians were a horse mounted people who lived on the grassland north of the Black Sea and the Caspian Sea. They called the Caspian Sea - the Sea of Raven. They were an Iranian people, often with blond or red blond hair. Many of them had blue eyes and in many ways,

they resembled the Nordic people. They were eminent horse people, and very capable warriors.

"They were pleased with colors and often decorated themselves and their horses with beautiful designs.

"Our people traded and fraternized freely with them."

"What happened then?"

"A horde of very cruel warriors arrived from further east. They were led by a man called Attila. They were extremely savage toward their enemies and spread terror in their wake. The Scythians were no match for them, and the Scythians then pressured our people to migrate south and west."

"How dreadful!"

"But now, my child, this is time for us to eat, and your little ears have heard enough for today. We may continue tomorrow."

"How do you know all this history, grandmother?" Thorhilde asked.

"We Vikings are not ignorant people. These stories have been retold throughout generations from grandparents to grandchildren. It is my solemn duty to enlighten your mind and understanding by making you aware of your bloodline and family history and even to prepare you for your destiny.

"Come let us eat! Do you want lefse or ordinary bread? We also have broth and fish. We will have milk to drink."

"I love lefse and fish."

Gyda is swaying a little and Thorhilde can see that she is in pain. Her old and frail body has endured so much labor and so much pain. Anyone can see that she is in need of assistance sometimes.

"What is wrong grandmother?" Thorhilde asks her.

"Nothing much, my dear child, this is just life" her grandmother answers.

"I will stand by you and help you as long as you need me!" the young girl blurted out.

"That is very nice of you, Thorhilde, but you will have your own life to live and I will only become a burden to you."

"No way! You will teach me everything that you know and I will be your eyes, your ears, and your legs and arms as long as you need me."

"Well, if so, why don't you start by doing my hair? But let us eat first."

They ate in silence after Gyda had blessed the food. They rolled the ready cooked cod in lefse and consumed it with milk. It was a very nutritious and delicious meal.

Now she was ready to assist her grandmother to undo, comb and brush her long hair. The old lady sat herself on a stool by the bed and asked Thorhilde to start to undo it. She had her hair set up in a bun on the back of her head with hairpins. When undone, it reached to below her waistline. Though greyish with some white streaks in it, it was shining and beautiful due to daily brushing.

Thorhilde combed it carefully before she brushed it with a beautiful looking brush that Gyda had received as a wedding gift. It had been brought to them by a merchant from Bergen and had been very expensive.

When she was done, she helped her grandmother to bed, and knelt down by her bedside and prayed with her for the well-being of their families, their animals and their crops. Her grandmother also reminded her to pray for wisdom and courage, as well as protection against evil. "Also please pray for the well-being of our priests and the poor and sick among us," Gyda admonished Thorhilde.

Thorhilde kissed her grandmother goodnight and went to her own bed to sleep.

She awoke early the next morning and as usual she bent down by her bedside and prayed to the Lord for His protection, for herself and for her grandmother, whom she felt was her duty to look after during the years that Gyda still had to live. Although the old Lady was very frail, she had amazing willpower and an abundance of wisdom and knowledge about almost everything.

Thorhilde thought to herself that we are really an excellent pair together; I have the strength of my youth, while she has the knowledge and wisdom of the old.

As always, when she awakened, she was in a good mood. She sang to herself as she admired the flowers that surrounded their settlement while sitting on the door tram. As the wise girl that she was, she inherently understood that laziness and idleness would prevent her from reaching the full potential of her life.

After her morning wash, she started her day with her daily chores. First, she made sure that all the dishes, tables and kitchen surfaces were thoroughly cleaned before she swept the floor with a broom. Even while

4

doing this, she was singing aloud and giving thanks to the Lord in her mind for having a good home, enough food and a loving grandmother to share her life with.

"How are you this morning, my little Sunshine?" she heard from the door of the chamber. Her grandmother entered the room smiling and happy looking.

"Very well, grandma! Did you sleep well also?"

"Of course, I did. I always do."

Thorhilde was not so sure that her grandmother was always completely honest with her. Once, when she awoke during the night, she could hear Gyda crying and sobbing. At first, she thought of entering her chamber, but because of her innocent wisdom, she understood that if her grandmother really wanted to share her grief with her, she would let her know.

"My little Sunshine, can you please help me set up my hair? The pins are on the little table by my bedside."

While doing her hair, Thorhilde asked her grandmother, "Later on today, will you please tell me more of the story of what happened to the Nordic tribes? I have become very interested in knowing about my origin."

"Then, today I will start with your mother, Thorgunn. She was of noble birth directly of Clan McDonald and Clan McLeod of the beautiful island of Sky of the inner Hebrides, on the west of the Scottish mainland. She was also a direct descendant of the High King of Ireland, as well as, the king of Norway, all in legal lineages of marriage.

"Thorgunn was a beautiful looking woman, her hair was black and shiny, like a raven, and she had glistering eyes like yours. She was not only good looking, but also was a beautiful inner woman with a heart of gold. You resemble her in many ways, but you do not have her raven black hair. Yours is a more golden blond, maybe from your Scythian ancestors."

"How did she die so early?"

"Her body was not all that strong, and giving birth to you became too much for her. Sadly, she was in labor for several days and she died shortly after giving birth to you, her only child."

"So, she died so that I could live?"

"Knowing you, my girl, it was worth it.

"You never knew her in this life, my little Sunshine; grief is felt differently in losing a lifelong companion or someone that you have come to love very much."

"Have you experienced that, Grandmother?"

"We will talk about that later.

"You also never met your father, Arnfinn. He was on board a merchant ship that sank in the cruel and brutal waters between Iceland and Greenland. They were on a voyage to Bergen to trade commodities for our settlement, when the ship disappeared between our settlement here in Northwest Greenland and Reykjavik in Iceland. It was a very sad story to tell your mother while she was childbearing with you. The poor woman was stricken with grief.

"Your father was my favorite son, and even now, I sometimes grieve for him. He was a sturdy and very handsome looking man, full of energy and easy laughter.

"Through me you are a direct descendant of Thorhilde, the wife of Eric The Red, who first colonized Greenland. Hence, you are also a direct descendant of Eric. I am glad that you are able to control your temper, which you must have inherited from him. You probably know that he was outlawed twice for murder, first in Norway, and then in Iceland."

"That's awful! Please continue!"

"Well, you asked me to tell you about the fate of the Caucasian settlements.

"Are you listening?"

"Yes, of course I am, grandmother. Please continue!"

"Many, many centuries ago, the tribal chief, Odin, had chosen Viking, his younger son, to lead the migration of the Nordic tribes, instead of his older son, Thor. Thor became infuriated with anger and swore that he would avenge this great injustice to his birthright. Thor left their Caucasian settlement by the Sea of Raven in his chariot, pulled by two vicious looking large rams, screaming and cursing in anger.

"Viking now became the leader of some of these Caucasian tribes, which would become the Nordic tribes. He was advised by Odin, who was stricken by age, to follow the North Star for their main direction after they had crossed the Bosporus Straits between Asia Minor and Europe.

"When they arrived at the straits, they were met by Princess Pulcheria, who was now in charge of the government, while her brother, Flavius Theodosius II, was on a journey to Ravenna in Italy on state affairs. She first invited Viking and the tribal elders to Constantinople, the capital of the Eastern Roman Empire on the west side of the straits.

"The capital city was a splendor to watch, fantastically decorated buildings with broad paved streets, where they could run their chariots. They had even built a large stadium, where chariot teams competed. Most of the people of Constantinople were either spectators, or they were betting on the results. Viking and the elders were invited to one of the events and the atmosphere was electrifying. They all had their favorites.

"The crossing of the Bosporus must have been a beauty to watch. A very strong surface current was running from the Black Sea toward the Marmara Sea and through the Dardanelles toward the Aegean Sea and eventually, to the Mediterranean Sea. Near the bottom of the straits, a saltier and colder current flows in the opposite direction.

"The surface current was of such magnitude that their first thought was to ferry them over, but they suddenly became in a hurry when they received an urgent message from Princess Pulcheria that her brother, the Emperor, was seen nearing the city. She could not vouch for what he might do when he learned that she had befriended them, and she advised them to hurry across the straits.

"Instead of using ships, they floated their wagons across the straits by tying inflated leather bags to them and having their swimming oxen pull them.

"All animals can swim by instinct, but sheep are very poor swimmers and will only endure some fifteen minutes in cold water before they sink. To help them swim across, they first sheared them of their wool, since their wet wool would weigh them down. Also, to prevent the current from taking the sheep too far down the straits and in that way making their stay in the water too long, they floated their wagons close to the sheep and downstream from them to prevent the sheep from drifting away.

"All the shepherd boys were also in the water with the sheep, encouraging them and assisting them in every way possible.

"Finally, they all crossed over, and a messenger from the Princess advised them to continue northward as soon as possible. If the Emperor were to hear of their crossing and should want to pursue them, then she would try to do everything she could to delay him.

"She wished them good luck on their further journey north.

"Well, this is enough for today, my girl" Gyda said. She was almost worn out telling the story, as if she could have been there with them.

Thorhilde had been listening in awe and with amazement. "How do you remember everything grandmother?"

"Our ancestors have always relayed these stories from generation to generation, some families better than others. Those families who really respected their ancestors saw to that the young people were told, often over and over again.

"But, now I am worn out by story telling and have to rest for a while. Tomorrow is Laugardag and after we have had our weekly bath and washed our clothes and cleaned our houses, I will tell you of the journey of our ancestors through Europe toward Jutland."

Thorhilde spent the rest of her day reflecting and pondering upon everything that her grandmother had told her. She especially pondered what her mother would look like when they would meet again in the next life. What would they have in common, and how would they be different. She knew very well that she had to control her temper; she knew what her ancestor, Eric The Red, had done.

The priest of the settlement had once told her that the weaknesses we had in this life would be with us in the next life unless we try to change our behavior. He had also made it clear to her that if she would live a good life on this earth, then she would be allowed to join her own mother and father in the next life. Later on, if she should have a family of her own, it would be similar for them.

In the Laugardag morning, Thorhilde helped her grandmother prepare the newly cleaned clothing, as well as the towels and sheet for the bath. They always fired the bathroom stove, even in summer time to make it cozy and avoid taking cold. In these Northwestern Settlements, all farms had saunas.

Thorhilde and her grandmother shared their sauna together. She helped Gyda undress and even had to lift her into the pool, as well as give her a hand in scrubbing herself. They were so close in heart that it did not seem to embarrass either of them. After they had washed and dried themselves, they sat together in silence for a long time, just feeling the atmosphere and the loving spirit between them.

Coming back to the house, Thorhilde helped her grandmother make boiled cod for dinner. They ate it with a stew of local roots and herbs. For dessert, they had berries and milk.

After Gyda had rested for a while, she supervised Thorhilde on how to clean the clothes they had taken off the night before.

"Some of the clothes we can boil," she said, "and some we will wash by hand, while others we are extremely cautious with, like wool or fine linen."

They fired up a large cauldron in the washing house and soaped their more coarse clothing with homemade soap made from sheep mutton. Gyda instructed Thorhilde to treat the woolen clothes with the utmost caution. "Wash it with only a little soap in lukewarm water. Never ever twist it, but only gently press most of the water out of the cloth. Then, dry it on a table, but first, roll it into a towel to extract most of the remaining moisture, and finally, dry them lying flat on a table. Never hang them up before they are completely dry.

"Woolen socks, mittens, hats, trousers, jackets and even woolen underwear have many times in our history saved not only lives, but also saved our limbs from being amputated. Wool has the unique feature of keeping the body warm even after becoming wet.

"Now, my little Sunshine, we will have a little rest before we clean the house."

They seated themselves on a stone bench in front of the house and admired the beauty of the land around them. Before them was the wide and majestic looking fjord with even more majestic looking mountains beyond, decorated with green pastures full of summer flowers. There were a few trees and some bushes and the grazing cattle seemed to be in a complete harmony with nature.

The top of the mountains were usually decorated with snow caps and it looked like a wonderland.

"We have our sheep, goats and some of our larger cattle on our summer pasture in our mountains, called setrer, similar to what they do in Norway," Gyda told Thorhilde.

"One day, you will be asked to participate in the milking and caring for these animals."

They came back into the house, and both seated comfortably before Gyda started her storytelling again.

"When our ancestral tribes crossed the straits of Bosporus, Princess Pulcheria provided a guide, who also brought them a warning message from the princess, 'Watch out for Attila! He recently tried to storm Constantinople with forty thousand horsemen. Because he didn't succeed, he sacked all the European lands in revenge.'

"Their guide led them to the river Maritsa which flowed southeast from an old city called Serdica, being one of the first cities in the world to fully embrace Christianity.

"When they arrived there, they found the city destroyed, looted and shamed with only a few survivors, who told them that Attila and his murderous band of horsemen had recently passed by on his way north. 'Attila is no respecter of human beings, and seems to be full of hatred for anything that even resembles Christianity or civilization in general,' the survivors told Viking.

"The Nordic tribes continued northward, now following the river Moravia through northern Macedonia and Serbia until it emptied into the great river Danube. From there, they followed the river Sava toward the Alp Mountains. With a tremendous effort, they managed to drive their wagons through one of the mountain passes and they arrived in the southern part of Germania.

"At this time, the entire Roman Empire was in big trouble, due to internal strife and the murderous attacks from the Huns, under their leader, Attila. South Germany had already been sacked and Viking was warned that unless you pay a large voluntarily tribute to Attila, he will definitely come after you.

"Where will I find him?" Viking asked.

"He has made Hungary his home and is holding a court there," he was told. "It may be wise to go and see him, bringing all your gold and valuables with you. That would perhaps spare your life."

"Viking conferred with his elders and they all understood the gravity of the situation. They would be practically defenseless against the thousands of trained horsemen.

"Hence, the very next day Viking and a few of his elders collected a large amount of gold and jewelry and, as advised, followed the river Danube southeastward toward Hungary. On the third day of travel, they met a small group of horsemen who quickly surrounded them, and

Viking gestured that he was traveling to meet with Attila, and that he had brought a tribute with him.

"They were escorted to Attila's camp, where he was sitting outside a large blue tent. He appeared to be sitting in a squatted position, eating. They quickly dismounted and brought him their tribute.

"The Huns were obviously of Mongolian decent. They had pale brown faces with small slanted eyes. Many of them had bare torsos that were decorated with blue and black tattoos. Because their faces were also tattooed, they were a fierce looking lot.

"The Nordic tribesmen saw immediately why they were such excellent horsemen. They and their horses were similar in shape.

"Viking asked for permission to travel north to Jutland, and Attila inquired why they wanted to do so, whereby Viking explained that it was their prophetic destiny. Then, Attila asked Viking if he had brought him everything they had of gold and jewelry, whereupon Viking told Attila that some of their women were still wearing a few of their most cherished possessions.

"Surprisingly, Attila seemed to like that answer, and said that he admired their honesty and their courage. He declared loudly, 'I also follow a prophetic destiny, like yours. Go your way in peace.'

"Viking retraced the Danube to the southern part of Germania, where his followers had been waiting, and led his Nordic tribes further north, following the river Danube toward the river Regen, where Regensburg is situated today. The Romans called it Castra Regina and it was one of their frontier cities along the river Danube. It is also one of the oldest cities in northern Germania, a very beautiful city, and also to their good fortune, it had a very helpful and enlightened Governor.

"The Governor told Viking that it had been a very wise decision to pay tribute to Attila, since he was infamous for his cruelty toward anyone in his way. He explained, 'Even this fortified and strong city is not safe from him. He has purchased siege weapons and siege knowledge from those with such knowledge, and many Goths have already joined with him, together with many other people from all over Europe. If he comes here, I would rather pay him the demanded tribute instead of risking the destruction of my city and my people. Hopefully, he will be busy somewhere else, so that we may not need to do so.'

"Although you are very welcome to stay with us," he told Viking, "I would advise you to travel north as soon as you can in order to avoid him. Even if you have paid tribute to him, he might demand that you and your people join him."

"Viking counseled with his elders, and they all agreed upon a speedy journey northward.

"After a month of difficult travel in heavy terrain, they came to the river Elbe that divides the Saxons from the Wenders. The Governor of Regentsburg had informed them that the Saxons had been asked by the King of England to settle the south of England in order to protect England against the Scots from Ireland, and the Picts from Scotland, who might decide to invade England in the wake of the Roman desertion of the island. The King had also requested the Angels who lived in South Jutland to migrate to Eastern England to assist him.

"Viking's tribes stayed on the western banks of the river Elbe in order to avoid the Wenders and only crossed over the river just before its estuary to travel further north . Eventually, they arrived at West Jutland and were well received by the Hardruders, who were also in the process of making a large migration to what was to become Norway.

"Now, my little Sunshine, this is surely enough for today. We both have to go to bed soon in order to be prepared for church tomorrow."

They prayed together kneeling by Gyda's bed. Thorhilde saw to it that her grandmother was comfortable without humiliating or embarrassing her. She understood well that her grandmother, even though being old and frail and in need of help sometimes, did not need to be treated like a child. She acted in a way that Gyda could keep her dignity and pride intact.

"Grandmother, I am so glad that you are here with me to teach me of everything, especially of our ancestors. It is amazing to me that you remember so well all these events that happened so long ago."

"I have been told over and over again by my grandmother, who was told by her grandmother over and over again. Even though my body is frail, my memory is still clear. Will you stay by me, my little Sunshine, until I leave to go to my ancestors?"

"Of course I will grandmother!" Thorhilde said with a sobbing voice. "I will never leave you for anything in this world."

"I know that you mean this now my child, but I also suppose that you will meet a nice man who wants to marry you. What then?"

"If he loves me, then he will love you too! If not, I will not have him!"

"We have prayed; let us try to get some sleep. Good night, my child. I love you."

"I love you too, Grandma! Goodnight and sleep well."

They went to the church the next morning at eleven am, Sunday. The church was not too far from their farm, only half an hour walk. Outside, they socialized with friends and neighbors before entering the church building.

The church was several hundred years old and was built mainly of stone and turf, due to the scarcity of wood. However, the altar was made of wood, as well as, the pulpit. They were both beautifully carved, the same way as was always done in the Norwegian churches.

The service was in Latin and very ritualized. Thorhilde was sitting next to her grandmother in a very dignified and respectful manner. She clearly felt the need the settlers had for the word of God in this lonely and harsh environment. The height of the Sunday ritual was always to partake of the communion. As she was now twelve years old, the priest had told her that she was eligible to partake, and that if she felt that she had done any wrong, then she should confess to the Lord through him as a mediator.

She partook of the communion with respect and awe.

When they came back to their house, Gyda treated Thorhilde with a distinctly Norwegian dish, called lutefisk. The settlers knew from the old land how to prepare it, and they all loved it. The fjord was full of fish waiting to be caught and eaten by the settlers.

"Today, we do not work" Gyda told Thorhilde as she had mentioned to her many times "unless there is an emergency or we have to.

"We will recite the commandments every Sunday afternoon to be sure that we do not treat them lightly or ever forget them" Gyda admonished Thorhilde. "Also, we will wear our Sunday clothes all day as a token of respect to our Heavenly Father. Will you start, Thorhilde, reciting the commandments for me please? Start with number one and say each of them in numerical order."

Thorhilde recited the first commandment "Thou shalt have none other gods before me."

"Very good, my girl, please continue."

Thorhilde recited them all correctly, reverently and in order.

"Thank you, my child. The Lord will protect you for all your good doings. You are a very good Christian girl, and smart and knowledgeable as well. I will also help you find a good husband! Will you allow me to do that?"

"Please do so, grandmother, your love for me would help you."

Chapter II

Preparation for departure - 1320

The men who have come together at the Lysu Farm were all in a very somber mood. They were called together by their parish priest, Guttorm, to discuss matters of extreme seriousness.

Guttorm, was both a large and a great man. He had a posture like an emperor and a mind like a saint. He was highly respected and liked by everyone in the Northwestern Settlement. He had a large greyish beard that he dressed in an immaculate way, and it protruded like a hammer when he was giving a sermon, officiating at an ordinance or especially when he became exited or angry.

Now, the men could all see that he was very serious, as well as excited but sorrowful.

He started calmly but in a sorrowful voice, "It grieves my heart to tell you the very sad news that I have heard and that I, as a loyal servant to the church and also to the King of Norway, need to report to you, my friends, my parishioners and my fellow men in Christ.

"The news that I have received represents demands for both increased taxation and increased duties, which will be paid to both the royalty and aristocracy in Norway, as well as to the leaders of our church in Norway.

"It has sadden me terribly to see that my own church, which I dearly love, is becoming more and more worldly. Now, in these difficult times, our church seems to have become more of a servant to the King and the aristocracy of Norway, than a servant of the Lord. This desire for riches seems to be true even for the leaders of our church, who now are mainly creating security for their own families, with positions and land for their own selfish interest, rather than serving the true and living God.

"My Christ-like concern for you is much higher than the loyalty that I have sworn to the bishop at Gardar, on behalf of the archbishop of Nidaros in Norway or even to the Pope himself in distant Rome. My concern for your welfare is higher than the loyalty that we all have sworn to the King of Norway.

"However, today, the King of Norway seems to have no real concern for us, but only wants to exploit our trading commodities when needed. What grieves me even more is that the bishops have become even worse than the King. They who portray themselves in fine clothing and symbols of authority and faked love for us, have become increasingly more and more wealthy, by robbing the poor and the widows of their possessions, farms and honor in many sly ways of disguise.

"My fellow men, I want you to seek among yourselves an able man or woman who can lead us across the waters to the south, for there we can settle in a land of liberty, like that which we had here earlier.

"The Norwegian aristocracy is coming too close to us and we do not need to carry them on our shoulders.

"In order to avoid confusion, we need an able leader in order to prepare for a structured emigration southward. I admonish you to seek out this leader before we leave, and crown him or her to lead us as either a King or a Queen.

"As much as I dislike royalties and all their privileges, I think it is a necessity today. Let there be no one who is heir to the throne after this regent. I am a practical man, as well as a servant of the Lord, and I think that this is the wisest way for our community.

"Go home now, all of you, and think it through. Discuss it with friends and neighbors and most important of all, ask the Lord in solemn prayer for His advice regarding both the migration and your choice of a King or Queen to lead us."

The men were all stunned and in awe. They had great respect for their parish priest and no one thought lightly of his advice and admonishment.

When Gyda heard the news from her neighbor, she called Thorhilde, now twenty-four years old, to her and said: "I knew that this was going to happen. Guttorm and I have talked about this a few times. Prepare yourself for the coming years, my dear. A lot of great responsibilities will be placed upon your shoulders."

"What do you mean grandmother?"

"We will talk more about that later."

Thorhilde knew very well that when her grandmother said it that way, it was final, so she did not argue with her, both out of respect and reason.

"Grandmother, tell me more about your life in Norway?"

"Well, I have been seriously ill for the last ten years, and you know that I would not even be here today had it not been for your loving care and strong arms and legs. In this season, I am in fairly good health, thanks to you, my Sunshine, and the will of the Lord.

"What do you want to know about Norway?"

"I want to know everything, how our Nordic ancestral tribes came there, how they settled in, their customs and joys, as well as sorrows."

"Some eight hundred years ago, our tribe, together with the Hardruders, sailed north in the North Sea from West Jutland to Norway. After a week of sailing against the wind, we settled with them in an area of Norway that still bears their name, Hardanger. Hardanger means the fjord of the Hardruders. Later on, the Hardruders became known as Hords, which gave name to Hordaland.

"There were some terrible battles that took place in the fjords before those invading tribes managed to secure their footing in the new land."

"That was horrible! Did they really have to kill other people in order to settle?"

"Well, they were viciously attacked and they had to defend themselves.

"Later on, our people moved further inland to the area of Voss and spread out in a peaceful manner throughout most of the country.

"Of course, our tribal ancestors sometimes intermarried with the original local inhabitants of the land, but they usually chose partners from within their own tribe for many years to come."

"What were those original people of Norway like?"

"They were somewhat different from us, and not as well organized as we were. Consequently, the local Princes were often chosen from our tribes, probably also because of their wisdom and integrity, as well as their good standing within their local communities."

"What were their farms like?

"They followed local building traditions and their farms were usually very large, with several buildings on them. They often built the dwelling house connected to the shed for the animals in order to receive some of the heat from the animals in their dwelling house.

"They would have a smithy and a woodworking shop, a storage shed for food and a storage shed for fire wood, as well as a barn and, of course, a sauna. They also had storage places for hay and grain. In addition, the farms would usually have a summer pasture house, called a seter, and a boatshed."

"This is very much the same that we have here today!"

"True!

"The most important animals were, of course, sheep, cows, pigs, goats and horses. They always had dogs to guard their sheep against attacks from bears and wolves, while on their summer mountain pastures. And they also had cats to keep rats and mice away from their houses."

"Did they keep their dogs and cats as pets?"

"No. They only had dogs and cats for the purpose of being useful to them."

"I still love cats, grandmother! Why don't we have one?"

"A cat would only become a problem for us, my dear. Let me think of it for a while."

The men of the Northwestern Settlement spent several days and nights pondering the seriousness of the fate of the settlement, as well as their loyalty oath to their King and their love of their church.

They knew that it was treason, punishable with death to do the thing that Guttorm the parish priest had proposed. However, they also knew that if they stayed, it could be a slow and embarrassing death to the settlement.

Summers were becoming shorter and shorter and the wheat that they sowed would usually not ripen. Even their barley hardly managed to ripen for them. The merchant ships from Bergen had even become more and more scarce, due to the competition from Lubeck in Wendland.

Signs were alarming and the dire future of their settlement was obvious for the men of the settlement to see. And when even their Parish Priest, a devout man of God, whom they all had complete confidence in, strongly advised them to forsake the Kingdom of Norway and settle in an unknown continent far to the south of them, what were they to do?

Their minds were troubled and they counseled with their wives, and even older children as well, so that their decision would be unanimous. Of course, they knew somewhat of the land to the south already. They had traveled some of that land and sailed some of those rivers for centuries already.

But for the whole settlement to leave? It was a frightening thought!

Gyda was well informed of their mental struggle and had her own mind made up. She was in complete agreement with Guttorm.

She relayed her feelings to Thorhilde and said to her "Whatever happens, my child, be willing to accept the responsibilities that you will be asked to take upon you. Will you promise me to do so?"

"What you are asking me is of grave concern, grandmother. But, I will undertake whatever I will be asked to do," she promised her grandmother.

"Tell me more about Norway, grandmother!"

"In Norway there are many mountains and fjords, but unlike here, there were also large forests. There were also many strange creatures living In the forests of Norway. Most dreadful were the trolls. They were the very first inhabitants of Norway and they did not like any human beings, especially the Christians.

"The trolls usually lived deep in the Norwegian forests and when they heard about a newborn human child, they would do their utmost to kidnap the child, and take it with them and bring it up as their own."

"This is really frightening, grandmother! Did they actually succeed in that?"

"Unfortunately, they were successful a few times, so the story tells us. But parents were very concerned and saw to that their children were christened as early as possible, before the newborn child came to the knowledge of the trolls, so their child would be protected."

"Good!"

"However, young men could also be lured away by some beautiful female creatures called Huldrer. They looked almost like a human being, except that they had tails like the trolls. The Huldrer had their hiding places deep in the forest.

"Some young and innocent young men became so enhanced by their beauty that they forgot that they had been warned by their mothers, and they followed an enticing Huldrer into the kingdom of the trolls."

"What would happen to them?"

"Well, they would become the servants of the trolls for eternity."

"Could they never come back again to their parents and families?"

"Sometimes they could, if their families would donate an estate or a large sum of money to the church!"

"Oh!"

"There were also other strange creatures that were after young and innocent children, like the Fossekallen that usually lived under the highest and most dangerous falls in the rivers. They would try to lure young children close to the falls by making strange sounds. If the child became curious and came too close to the falls, they were doomed. The Fossekallen would grab them and take them in behind the falls and keep them as his children."

"This is horrible! Didn't the parents warn their children?"

"Of course, but children don't always listen to or obey their parents."

"I would have been very careful around the falls, grandmother"

"I know that you would have been, Sunshine!"

"Then, we also had Draugen that lived deep down in the forest lakes of Norway. He is a very weird creature and is very seldom seen or heard of. However he is as dangerous to the young and innocent as both the trolls and Fossekallen.

He would drag his victim down to the bottom of the lake, where he has his home, and keep them there forever."

"Oh, how frightening!"

"Yes, it certainly is, and the parents warned their children again and again to stay away from the forests lakes, especially those quiet lakes far into the forest where it is likely that Draugen would be.

"Also, there were Gnomes in Norway that mostly lived close to or even inside the farmhouses by night to keep warm.

"If the farmers were not nice to them and would not give them some food or milk, then they would avenge them by either having the cows stop giving milk, or having the animals becoming sick."

"Did the farmers help the Gnomes?"

"If they were wise, they did, and they prospered. The Gnomes could also assist the farmers in many ways, for example by doing some labor for him by night, unseen.

"Also, I will mention one more very strange creature, half human and half fish. The Mermaid had an upper body like a woman and the lower body like a fish. When she hid her lower body under the water and only showed her upper body to the sailors and fishermen, she could often lure them after her into the sea, where she could drown them and take them with her deep down into the ocean. Because she was so beautiful looking, she has lured many young sailors with her into her kingdom."

"How dreadful, grandmother. Did you know anyone who was lured away?"

"No, but I have heard of several that I didn't know. Enough for now, my Sunshine, we will soon have other things to talk about."

Guttorm called for the settlers to assemble again, this time outside the church and he has invited everyone, even the little children.

He started by leading everyone in a solemn prayer to the Lord and asking for His counsel and protection. After the prayer, he started,

"My fellow settlers, friends and neighbors, I have given the matter that I relayed to you not long ago a lot of sincere prayer, and a lot of deep contemplation. I have also counseled with many of you, but I will not dwell so much on the injustices that have been given us by the kings, the aristocracy, the bishops and the Southeastern Settlement. Instead, I will talk about our future and the possibilities that every new day offers us, if we are willing to shoulder the responsibilities that the Lord opens up for us.

"The time has come for us to prepare for the migration to the continent to the south of us. That land is ready to receive us, new settlers with a willing mind and a desire to help each other. There are people there that we can work together with as friends, and with whom we can even assist in every way that we are capable of.

"However, before we can leave this settlement, we need to build another twenty smaller ships, so that we can all stay together when we migrate. To do so, we need lots of building material and some time. We have the knowledge to build these ships, as well as the tools that we will need. But, we will need to travel extensively to Markland because that is where there is the timber that we need. To stay in Markland and build the ships there would be too dangerous for us.

In Markland, we would have to be constantly on guard for long periods of time, and be far away from our secure homes. This means that it would take several years to build our additional needed ships, but building them here will be a much safer approach.

"Hence, we will need to bring back the timber for building our ships. When we are building our ships here, we will need to do it in secrecy and in such a way that any visitors from Norway or the Southeastern Settlement will not be aware of it, in order to avoid arousing their curiosity or suspicion.

"We will need able men and ships to do this and we must do this during the short summers when the sea is more calm and we can travel more safely. We will need some twenty men and at least two ships to start cutting and freighting the timber for the building of the ships immediately. I am asking for one able unmarried man from each full farm, as well as experienced sailors to come forth."

The men were as astonished this time as they had been earlier of his bravery and foresight and diligent planning.

"What is the hurry?" one of the men asked.

"Time is the most important asset that we have," answered Guttorm. "I do feel that we must act now!"

"Have you inquired of the Lord?" The same man queried again.

"Yes I have. Many times. And the answer is always the same. Leave this settlement for the continent to the south and find the freedom that you yearn for.

"If you doubt what I have told you, you should also ask the Lord?" Guttorm replied.

Many of the other men urged the man to be quiet. They had too much respect for their Parish Priest to speak openly against him in public.

Nevertheless, many of them did have their own doubts about the whole matter.

After a few moments of murmuring, about ten young men did step forward to volunteer in answer to Guttorm's plea. Six experienced sailors also volunteered.

"That number will have to do, Guttorm said. We will start early tomorrow morning. I will give you the Holy Communion today and I will also give you my blessing, as well as the blessing of the Lord to be with you.

"I will also expect everyone here not to tell any visitors about our plans, so that the King of Norway will not send his warriors after us. Also, we need to plan for the construction of our additional small ships and find a suitable hiding place in one of the desolate fjords for the finished and ready ships. We are all going to be very busy.

"Before I leave you today, I want to know if you are all united in one body with me. Are you?"

As he could clearly see, there were none against him, at least not openly.

After returning home, Gyda and Thorhilde sat in silence for a long time, before Gyda finally spoke.

"Well, what do you think of all this, Sunshine?"

"It is simply overwhelming!"

"Do you trust the judgment of our priest?"

"Yes, I do. He is a man of the Lord, an honest and a good man," Thorhilde said. "But, I do have a feeling that not everyone in the settlement is happy about this!"

"True, but they dare not go against Guttorm and the majority of the settlers. What else did you learn today, Sunshine?"

"That several of the young men came forward and volunteered to go to Markland, even tomorrow morning."

"You are an excellent observer, my girl. I also observed that the man that I hope that you will marry soon was the first man to volunteer!"

Thorhilde couldn't help blushing. "You don't mean that…."

"Yes, I do, I have been praying to the Lord about giving you advice about who to marry, and I got the answer that the first man to come forward after being admonished by Guttorm should become your husband. I knew beforehand that he would ask that question, and even though I was not sure before that moment, I became very convinced then. Do you like him, my granddaughter?"

"I don't know! I hardly know him. Do you really think that he will want me for a wife?"

"You will soon know! I will go and visit his parents, and Guttorm right away. If we have your consent, his consent, his parents' consent and the blessing of the priest you could become engaged to him even today!"

Thorhilde didn't know what she should or could say, but she did not question the wisdom of her grandmother.

As Gyda was approaching the home of Erling's parents, she admired the beauty of their settlement and her thoughts went back to her own engagement, forty years ago. When she was engaged, she was only seventeen years of age, and she was engaged to a man of thirty-five.

Even though she did not love him at first, she did not go against the will of her parents, and it turned out that their marriage became a success.

Erling, however, was of the same age as Thorhilde. He was handsome, strong and intelligent, with good and highly respected parents. Gyda was gracefully received by Erling's parents, and it didn't take them long to accept her proposal.

They called for Erling and he answered, "Yes," in the same second that he was asked.

Before leaving their home, they agreed to meet at Guttorm's house as soon as possible. When they all arrived there, Thorhilde could see in Guttorm's face that he had been informed by Gyda beforehand. The smile on his face as well as the glances between him and Gyda gave them away. Of course, for this ceremony and ordinance, they needed two witnesses, but they were already at hand. Every detail had been anticipated and preplanned by Guttorm and Gyda.

As they were leaving, Gyda said smilingly to Thorhilde, "Perhaps you should say hello to your espoused husband? You might even give him a little kiss!"

Thorhilde blushed and did not know what to say.

The couple was conveniently left alone for the rest of the night, but Thorhilde returned home at an appropriate time looking happy and innocent, and Gyda knew that she had been safe with Erling.

When the ship sailed for Markland the next morning, they were all there to say good bye, to loved ones and friends. The settlement was a very close knit community and everybody knew each other very well. They always managed to settle disputes and grievances between them in an amiable way before it came to angry feelings between them.

After coming back home, Thorhilde asked, "Grandmother, would you please tell me how they settled disputes between people in Norway?"

"Well, the Norwegian Vikings had a law system very early on, which they must have brought with them from Israel. Israel had a law system and a court to judge their laws, which was called the Sanhedrin. It was a court of wise elders, and it could only sit in counsel in daylight. At that time, most of the rest of the world outside of Israel was barbaric, to say it mildly.

"The oldest law in Norway is the Gulathing Law and it is more than five hundred years old. In the beginning, all free adult men who owned property could speak to the assembly, which was called the 'Thing.'"

"Why only them, what about the women or those that did not own any property?"

"Even with these restrictions, the Gulathing was the most fair in the whole of Europe. Also, if everyone were to meet together, there would be too many."

"You said, 'in the beginning.' Has the Thing changed?"

"Unfortunately, yes! As the Kings of Norway became more settled, rich and mighty, an aristocracy arose, within the royal family and even the church.

"They altered the rules for the Thing in such a way that only some handpicked, often very rich farmers could speak and vote at the Thing."

"What was the real purpose of the Thing?"

"To have the law read and studied, and to settle grievances and disputes between people, before they turned into family feuds or violence. If unresolved, those family feuds could tear the country to pieces."

"Would the men always respect the decision of the Thing?"

"In most cases, yes, but not always."

"What type of decisions could the Thing make?"

"In extreme cases, the Thing could issue a judgment for a death sentence, either by being beheaded with a sword or by being burned to death, for really evil doings.

"They could declare an individual an outlaw, as they did twice to your forefather, Eric the Red. This ruling is almost the same as a death sentence, since anybody could legally kill him, without fear of punishment.

"The court could issue fines. They could decide in property grievances and absolve people of certain charges. There were no way to imprison them or take their freedom of movement from them."

"What good did the church do when it was first established in Norway?"

"The first thing the church did, when it was widely accepted in Norway was to set all the slaves free. At that time, almost a third of the Norwegian population were slaves. When they became free, they had to settle on the poorest land."

"Grandmother, you told me that I might have inherited my red blonde hair from our Scythian ancestors, or from our Irish ancestors. Could you, please tell me more about that?"

"The Norwegian Vikings controlled large parts of Ireland for many years, due to the fact that the Irish were always preoccupied in a very destructive civil war, and they were not sufficiently organized to protect themselves against invaders.

"The Vikings easily admired the beauty of the redheaded Irish women and brought many of them back to Norway, with or without their consent, in order to marry them. A lot of Norwegian people, especially those in western Norway are either red headed or have red blonde hair like you.

"Are you already wondering about the hair color of your children?"

"Yes, I am!"

"Erling is dark haired, like most of the settlers here, so you might have some dark haired children and some red blonde!" Gyda says.

"That is probably true."

"Thorhilde, I am so happy for you. I have often prayed to the Lord that I should be allowed to live long enough to see you married, and to also hold my first great-grandchild. Really, I am perhaps even happier than you are now."

"Don't be too sure of that, grandmother" Thorhilde answered with a sly smile on her face, and Gyda knew in her heart that Thorhilde would be very happy in her marriage.

Guttorm again summoned the men and addressed them.

"The next few years before us will be of great importance to us. We are going to leave what is today a safe harbor and venture into the unknown wilderness of a vast new continent."

One of the men asked, in surprise, "You say unknown! But have we not traveled that land and sailed the great rivers of that land for centuries?"

Guttorm answered, "Our usual traveling routes are also well known to the Southeastern Settlement and, accordingly, to the bishop at Gardar, as well as the Archbishop at Nidaros, and the merchants of Bergen and, of course, to our greatest threat the King of Norway. In order to punish us, he might even send warriors after us, even into the wilderness.

"Hence, in order to find safety, we must find a new traveling route and safe, secure settlements among the friendly natives of that continent."

"But, where and how will we find that?" a man asked.

"Our old trading route goes from the Winnipeg River down the Mississippi River and over the Great Lakes to the Iroquois River. We must avoid that route," Guttorm replies.

"So, where will we settle?"

"There is an abundance of good virgin land further south, east and west. We can make that decision later," Guttorm replied.

"However, we will also need to prepare for becoming independent in the production of iron. We have become too dependent on importing iron from Norway. We need to start making iron the same way as they did in olden times in Norway. Fortunately, we still have men and women with us who know how to do it, and they will start teaching us how.

"Furthermore, we will need to train men, women and children in combat and the use of weaponry, so that we will be able to defend ourselves."

Chapter III

After Her marriage to Erling - 1324

Thorhilde and her grandmother are sitting quietly in their chairs in the living room of their farm. They are both in deep silence as they are both reflecting upon the past, the present and the future of their families and their loved ones, as well as their own destiny.

Thorhilde asked "I have wondered many times how it will be when I die. What will really happen to me?"

"You will find that out, my love! Good people like you have nothing to fear! Both your mother and your father will be there to greet you. Furthermore, I and my husband will greet you too. But, you will first meet your parents and your husband and your children, if they should happened to die before you."

"Oh, I really look forward to meeting all of you on the other side! It is almost too good to be true!"

"Yes, that is true, but we still have important work to do here on this earth before the Lord will allow us to leave."

"Of course, I do understand that, grandmother. But, please continue telling me your story about our ancestors. It has been a few years since you told me about their lives in Norway."

"It has been a few years, but you are a married woman now with two small children, and you have been very busy with many other things that you have had to attend to. However, since your husband is away on a voyage to Markland to bring back building materials for our ships, and since both of your two children are sleeping in bed, I will continue.

"After our people had been deported to The Caucasus and had stayed there for one thousand years, they were advised by Odin to follow the North Star to their destiny far to the north. There, he told them, they would be safe.

"Actually, we lived well in that country for four hundred years more until overpopulation and the stern rule of Harald Fairhead encouraged settlers to seek settlement in Iceland.

"Iceland is not a land with beautiful pastures and lush forests. Instead, it is treeless and has almost barren soil. Even so, many settlers followed that adventure and they choose the name, Iceland, to discourage too many others from overrunning the island.

"After about a hundred years in Iceland, the island had no more tillable land, and some of the growing population became restless.

"Because of a storm at sea, a ship that was bound for Iceland had come further west, and they lived to tell of a large land, perhaps an island, with beautiful fjords, as well as green meadows and a milder climate than most of Iceland.

"Our forefather, Eric the Red, had come to Iceland as a refugee from the law. He had been outlawed in Norway for murder."

"Oh, did he really kill someone in Norway! How horrible! Why did he do such a thing?"

"Well, he had a terrible temper, and was often not in control of it. After coming to safety to Iceland, which didn't belong to Norway, he fell in love with your ancestral mother, Thorhilde, a devout and beautiful Icelandic woman of a good family. She had embraced Christianity and she tried, unfortunately in vain, to convert her husband, Eric, as long as she lived."

"That was sad. Maybe he will convert in the next life?"

"He will first have to pay for his crimes. He did murder two people, one in Norway and later one in Iceland, who had even given him refuge from the Norwegian law and punishment."

"Is it not fortunate that Eric was not executed? If he had been killed, maybe neither of us would be here!"

"That is so true, my girl. Perhaps none of our closest ancestors would have been born.

"After he had explored the West Greenland coastline for three years, Eric settled far southeast at a beautiful fjord that he called Ericsfjord, and he founded a large and beautiful farm called Brattali. It was a gorgeous place, with lots of free virgin land for newcomers to settle in. It was sheltered from the northerly wind, and there were plenty of fish and seals in the waters."

"Why are we not living in the Southeastern settlement now, grandmother?"

"Torfinn Karlsevne was the first settler here in this Northwestern settlement, and our ancestors choose this place too.

"Eric encouraged more people from Iceland to come to this land by giving favorable reports back, and even naming the land Greenland, to make it sound lush. I am getting tired, now, Thorhilde."

The next morning, Thorhilde faced the reality of motherhood.

Both of her two children were sick with measles. The older child is a boy called, Yngve, after Erlings father, and the younger daughter is called, Thorgunn, after Thorhildes mother.

Yngve is now three years old and Thorgunn has just turned one year of age.

They were both very sick. Yngve, especially, was not in very good general health. He is fairly timid for a boy, and Thorhilde has wondered many times how much longer she will have him with her, before she has to give him back to the Lord. He always have a pleasant smile on his face, even though he must be in great pain. It seems like he wants to convey a silent message to his mother through his shining eyes.

"Do not be afraid, my mother! We are now here together on this earth, perhaps for only a short time, but we will always be together for eternity!" Thorhilde could feel her eyes becoming full of emotion, and as she stretched out her hand toward her little boy, he grabbed her hand tightly and smiled sweetly.

She could not control her feelings now, and started crying softly, because she knew in her heart that her son does not have long time to live. Eventually, she had to force herself to let his hand go.

The eye contact between them in that brief moment had been of such a magnitude of love and understanding that it was beyond description.

Thorhilde had to find solitude and pray to the Lord.

She thanked the Lord deeply for giving her two beautiful children, a caring and responsible husband, and a loving and caring grandmother. She also thanked the Lord for good health, and a good home, and sufficient food.

"Dear Lord." she prayed, "if you are going to take this little boy from me, please make the days we still have together as enjoyable as possible." Even as Thorhilde was full of sorrow for her sick children, she was also aware of the realities of life, as well as the consolation from her Christian upbringing.

When she reentered the room, she found Yngve sleeping, smiling in his sleep. Her baby girl, Thorgunn, is healthier than her brother, and Thorhilde hopes that she will reach maturity.

Her grandmother has carefully advised her on how to care for her children, and she is doing her utmost to see to it that they get every care that may be done for them.

She often thinks of her husband, Erling. Due to the task that has been put on his shoulders, he has been away from her most of their married life. She also knows that when he comes home from Markland, Guttorm had asked him and some of the other sailors to sail some merchandise to Bergen in Norway for funding their migration. This unapproved trading is now illegal, because the King of Norway has established a trading monopoly between Norway and Greenland.

For many years, the Greenland settlements had been visited at least yearly, sometimes more often, by merchants from Bergen, but lately, there have sometimes been years between their visits.

Guttorm wanted to have first hand information on what was really happening in Norway, and he had complete confidence in Erling and the sailors that were to accompany him on this illegal journey. He informed them to trade for tools for iron making and shipbuilding, as well as tools for agriculture purposes and weapons.

The children were now sound asleep and Thorhilde went to see if Gyda needs any help.

"How are you, my Sunshine?" Gyda greets Thorhilde warmly.

"I am worried for Yngve and my husband, but still happy to be here with you, grandmother."

"We have to trust in the Lord, my dear; He always knows what is best for us. Is there anything that I can do for you to relieve your mind of your worries?"

"Please tell me about the early years of our settlements here in Greenland."

"Of course, I will.

"Where do you want me to start?"

"Start with our settlement."

"The oldest farm here is Sandnes, which was settled by Torfinn Karlsevne some three hundred years ago, not far away from us. Later on, many other settlers arrived from Iceland, where all the productive agricultural land had been taken.

"It was warmer then and the fjords provided an excellent shelter from the northerly storms. They improved their land in such a way that they could sow both wheat and barley. The farmhouses where constructed in the same manner as in Norway. They even had summer pasture houses for their animals, the same way as in the old country.

The fjords were full of salmon and cod, and there were many seals and whales to be hunted. It was almost a paradise for land hungry settlers. Merchant ships arrived regularly from Bergen to trade needed commodities and the price for walrus tusk was very good."

"Why was the walrus tusk so valuable, grandmother?" Thorhilde asked in astonishment.

"In Europe they made crucifixes, chess figures, ornaments of all kinds, walking stick handles, and a variety of other things from the walrus tusk.

"We also traded live falcons, which were in very high demand in Europe, as well as polar bear skins."

"That must have made this settlement somewhat wealthy?"

"Yes, things were going well for us all.

"Eventually, the land in this Northwestern settlement also became all taken with almost a hundred farms scattered around the adjacent fjords."

"What did they do then, grandmother? Would someone probably have to leave!"

"Many did leave and settled in the interior of the southern continent, most of them on the Missouri River, where the Mandan Nation live. There, they built a Viking style city among the friendly native Mandan tribe.

"Some of our settlers who migrated south also settled peacefully along the mighty Mississippi River, as well as on the large Ohio River, and some even as far south as on the Tennessee River. Some even settled on the west coast of the mighty continent, where the Tlingit's lived.

"The first one hundred and fifty years here, our settlements were very prosperous indeed. However, there were many children born who were hungry for their own farms, and they knew from hunters and traders that there was plenty of land to the south. Thousands upon thousands left our Northwestern settlement to find freedom and land of their own.

"Taxation wasn't as bad then. Greenland was not yet completely under the King of Norway and it took some time before a Bishop was appointed to Greenland.

"There was also free trade. In the early days, we could trade freely with anyone, and the merchants who came here from Bergen paid very good prices for our merchandise."

"That was fantastic, but did the people try to settle other places too?"

"Well, we also tried to establish some settlements on the big lakes, but we encountered problems with the Iroquois tribes, especially the Erie tribe, who lived on the south side of the second largest lake, not too far from the large waterfall that the natives call Niagara. Either we had to pay them a tribute, or we had to fight them. We did not fear them, but it became too much suffering for us to settle in that region.

"However, the Southern Settlement had a station of warriors at the Niagara Falls for some time in order to secure the bypassing of the falls for their trading ships"

"Do we keep in contact with those other settlements today?"

"Occasionally. But, times are not as good today as they used to be and it's a long journey to visit them!"

"That's understandable! But, what do you mean by saying that times are not as good today as before?"

"Well, mostly, taxation has become such a burden to us that we have become more like serfs, whereas we were a free people earlier."

"What do you mean?"

"Well, for example, we have to pay for permits to hunt whales, polar bears and polar foxes. Also, the Bishop is even heavily charging us for saying masses for our dead, as well as heavy charges for issuing the letters of indulgences. In addition to ordinary tithes, we were ordered to pay an extra tithe for the crusade of the Norwegian King Sigurd to the Holy Land.

"Because we are under the King of Norway, we were even ordered to assist him in his warfare, as well as paying even more taxes to uphold the newly established Norwegian aristocracy."

"That does not seem fair to us!"

"No, it was not fair. But, the worst is the aristocracy that developed in the Southeastern Settlement. The Bishop and the richest settlers there purchased expensive clothes and jewelry from the merchants of Bergen and established a new Greenland aristocracy. They became the most dangerous threat to us in our more humble settlement further west and north.

"They have imposed so much taxation on us, that, today, very few of us even own our own farms anymore. We have become tenants to a greedy church aristocracy.

"This is the main reason that so many of us have already left and have formed settlements to the south."

"I would like to meet with those people sometime!"

"Maybe you will get that chance before you know!"

"I am becoming very exited about this, grandmother!"

"The blood of your ancestor, Eric the Red, must flow through your veins in abundance. It is good to have goals, but it is also wise to make sober plans for accomplishing those objectives" Gyda said smilingly. "Now before we do anything we will see to the children."

The two women entered the two bedrooms silently and saw both children asleep, Yngve breathing somewhat heavily, while Thorgunn seemed more comfortable. Gyda comforted Thorhilde as gently as she could. She was fully aware of what might happen to Yngve soon, but tried as best she could to ease Thorhilde's burden by talking of something else.

"You know very well, Thorhilde, that in order for us to survive here in this desolate region of the world, we had to expand beyond the Southeastern settlement to our settlement. You have probably heard it said, 'The Vikings have the urge to explore foreign lands!'

"And this is very true.

"There are no other people on this very earth that have such a horizon of common knowledge and experience that we have!"

"But, grandmother, that sounds like bragging!"

"No, it is the truth!

"When all the land in our settlement was becoming taken, ships were first sent out to explore the northern parts of this continent. They came back with exiting news of having found large colonies of the precious walruses north and south of a passage to an ocean were the Aleuts live."

"Who are the Aleuts?"

"They are the natives of the Aleutian Islands, and they are really great hunters. The possibilities for trading with them opened up tremendous opportunities for the exchange of merchandise. They were friendly toward us and very curious. If you travel further south along the coast, they told us you would meet the Tlingit's and you will see all their fantastic wood carvings.

Also you may encounter a bear that is even larger than the Grizzly Bear!"

"What is a Grizzly Bear, grandmother?"

"Well, our explorers encountered the Grizzly Bear first when they were following the Saskatchewan River. It is twice as large as a Black Bear and twice as dangerous. It will attack any intruder on its territory with such ferocity that it is almost unthinkable. Even though it frightened our men, they were well armed and trained in both hunting and combat. But for a man by himself, even being armed, meeting a Grizzly Bear could be very dangerous."

"Aren't the Polar bears also dangerous, grandmother?" Thorhilde asked.

"The Polar Bears are also very strong and dangerous. The Polar Bears are more sly than the Grizzly Bears. They may hide behind some ice and make a surprise attack. Since they are white, they blend very well with the snow and the ice.

"Quite a few of our men have lost their lives in sudden encounters with the Polar Bears. It is far safer to trade with the Eskimos for their skins.

"In the beginning, we traded with the Inuit Eskimos to the north of us. They were happy to trade their walrus tusks, walrus hides and walrus meat for glass jewelry for their women, kitchen utensils, knives and other things. They also traded their polar bear skins and their polar fox skins.

"They live northwest of us around an island called Helluland. There are plenty of walrus all around that island. Before we even started trading with the Inuits, we hunted the walruses ourselves, but we soon discovered that it was far more profitable to trade.

"For almost three hundred years, we have sailed and traded in these waters, and there is not an island or a sound that we have not explored."

"Did some of our men fraternize with the Eskimos?"

"Well, they must have, because many of the Inuit's have Nordic features."

"So, they are our cousins!"

"Yes, they are indeed!"

Erling is now back from Markland, and he and Thorhilde are now able to share some precious time together. It has been so long since the last time that were together. There is a deep admiration between them, a mixture of love, understanding, respect and sense of shared duties.

They are both people of integrity and character with the best to be found. Both are also filled with love and compassion toward not only their own families but also, toward their neighbors.

They both know that their time together will be limited, because Erling is to depart for Bergen soon. The ship is already waiting for him.

Before leaving his home with Thorhilde, Erling says goodbye to his sweet children. Thorgunn is sleeping, but Yngve gazes at his father with a smile on his face, even though he is in great pain. The atmosphere is electrified, and Erling cannot stop, but starts crying.

He remembers what is said, "A guy doesn't cry!" But, he cannot console himself. Vividly, he feels that this is the last time that he will see his family all together. The tears stream freely down his cheeks and he doesn't try to stop them. Thorhilde see his grief and senses his embarrassment for crying in her presence.

At last, he manages to pull himself free from his emotions. He kisses both of them good bye, and little Yngve raises both his arms and pulls them tight around his father's neck as if to keep him there forever.

Thorhilde followed him silently to the ship.

She watched the ship sail and fastened her eyes on her husband until the ship slowly disappeared across the bay.

On her way back home, she walked as if in a trance. Her eyes were half-way shut, and she is almost about to fall just before she enters her home. Well inside the house, she lay down exhausted on her bed even too fatigued to undress.

This is the way that her grandmother finds her shortly thereafter. She gently strokes her hair, her brow and her arms. "You are not well now, my little darling," she said with motherly love. "Come, we will sleep together tonight. The children are both safe and asleep."

Gyda slips herself into her bed, puts her arms around her and tucks her into herself like a mother tucks a baby into herself. Thorhilde can now let her emotions flow freely and she starts crying openly with low moaning, until her eyes become sore and she eventually goes to sleep.

The next day, Thorhilde feels that with the help of her dear grandmother, she has been able to take control of herself again.

When the necessary chores were done in the house the next day, Gyda approaches Thorhilde and says "There is one thing that I have often thought of and that I have had news of lately.

"In Iceland, a very prominent local chief, Snorre Sturlasson, has written Sagas of our ancestors. I learned to read and write from the monks in the cloister of the Southern Settlement. I am able to both read and write Latin, as well as Nordic. I want to use this next year while your husband is away to teach you both languages, at least to give you a working knowledge of them. You are a very smart woman and will learn fast. Guttorm is also in command of both languages."

"Oh! That sounds interesting! When shall we start?"

"Why not immediately? I will bring books, papers and writing material in. Just wait my girl.

"We will start with Latin."

"Why not Nordic? Then I could read about our ancestors!"

"Latin is the most important, since it contains the word of God. We will start with the reciting of the commandments in Latin, until you first know them by heart, and then are capable of writing them correctly in Latin. How does that sound?"

"Good!"

"Then, we will start with the most common daily words, as well as the most important names that you might encounter, most of them related to church service and church ordinances.

"After we have finished your Latin lessons, you will be ready for your Nordic lessons.

"OK. You are already well acquainted with speaking Nordic correctly, and you will be in command of reading Nordic letters very soon. However, teaching you to write it correctly will be the most difficult task for us.

"In order to accomplish all this, we will have to study regularly and use any spare time that you have available. We will even have to recite and use it in our conversation when we do our daily chores. I am exited about starting now. Aren't you too?'

"Yes, I am grandma!"

"I am especially interested in reading the Icelandic Sagas! They will contain some of the family history of our ancestors. I can hardly wait!"

"Well, in order to get started, let us start with Latin. And, as I said, the first task is learning the commandments."

They read and recite, over and over again until Thorhilde has almost remembered all of them in Latin. Her grandmother tells her also over and over again, "The art of learning is to repeat, and to repeat over and over again."

"Why?" Thorhilde asks.

"Because we forget things, and we need to be reminded of them. We have to attend church over and over again too! Most of us are not all that spiritually strong, and without having the word of God recited to us over and over again, we wouldn't be able to live in tranquility, as we are doing here today."

"But, you are spiritually strong, grandmother!"

"Thank you, my dear, for saying so. But even being strong does not mean that we can do without the help of the Lord. Never forget, my little Sunshine, always stay close to the Lord and His commandments."

The year passes by and the men have been spending all of their free time working on the ships that are needed for the migration of the settlement to the new land further south. The ships are made for both the crossing of the straits to the south, as well as for the journeys on the rivers.

The ships are built to travel in shallow waters, as well as to hold a considerable amount of cargo, since the settlers are leaving with everything that they consider of value to them, including many of their animals. Any ocean voyage would be out of the question for them, but these ships will serve their purpose when they are all finished. Only one of the ships will be decorated, namely that ship, which will be the ship of their King or Queen.

These sailing ships may also be rowed and they are each equipped with eight pair of oars; except the largest one has sixteen pair of oars.

The largest ship will be decorated with a beautifully decorated dragon head on the front of the ship to show authority and to instill fright into any opponent. The Vikings of the Northwestern Settlement are very religious and do not see anything wrong in preserving their ancestral Norwegian culture and heritage.

The men are also supported and encouraged by their spouses, who bring them food and often keep them company while they are working. They sometimes bring their whole family along, even their children, and the whole atmosphere is joyful and inspiring to the men who are laboring. They all know that the small ships, or rather very large boats, are to transport them and also to house them for some time to come.

The men also know that it is of the greatest importance that the ships are sturdily built, so that they will all be safe on their journey. Each of the ships will be tested for seaworthiness and especially for water tightness before the start of their migration.

There is an unusual feeling of joy among them and most of the settlers have never felt anything like it before. They are all very happy and looking forward to their adventure. All opposition against the migration has completely died out.

Then, some terrible news arrives from the Southern Settlement. The ship which was sent to Bergen for trading of necessary commodities to the settlement has barely made it to Greenland. Due to very stormy weather, it arrived in horrible condition and needs to be repaired there before it can continue further north toward our Northwestern Settlement.

The days went by and the families who had crew members on board were all anxiously waiting for the small ocean going ship to arrive.

An atmosphere of doom was hanging over the settlement and it had completely replaced the earlier atmosphere of joy.

One day late in the fall, the little ship arrived and as it rounded the last corner of the fjord could be seen more clearly from where they were all waiting. As the ship came closer, they could all see clearly that it had been badly battered by the stormy sea.

Some of the railing was gone and the mast was severely damaged as well. An improvised rudder had been made to replace the old one that must have been broken off. As the men left the ship to come ashore, there were three of them who were missing, including Erling.

There was joy among those families that were reunited with their loved ones, but this was overpowered by the sad crying and wailing from those who were missing their beloved ones. Guttorm was desperately trying to console the families of the three missing sailors, but their sorrow was so deep that he could not reach them.

Thorhilde was looking at the scene in stunned silence. Inside her, she had already known. It was the same feeling that she had felt when she saw her husband leave. Only this time, she somehow managed to control herself better.

Instead of feeling sorry for herself, she went to see the families of the other two families and tried to share her grief with them.

They were told by the survivors that just as the ship was about to round the southern headland of Greenland and as they were in the middle of the East Greenland Stream, they encountered a mean storm with very heavy wind gusts from the southwest.

The powerful winds tore their sail to pieces in a moment and most of it was hanging over the starboard railing, which also threatened to take the rest of the sail, as well as the mast with it. Erling and the two other missing sailors immediately grabbed axes and started to chop away the damaged part in order to stabilize the ship again.

Just after they were done and as they were turning about northward with the stream, another heavy gust came and wiped the three men, as well as most of the starboard railing off into the sea. The men disappeared so quickly that in seconds they were too far from the ship with no chance whatsoever for the remaining crew to rescue them.

Thorhilde could see clearly that the remaining crew not only found it difficult to tell the families of the deceased men about their fate, but they were also carrying a burden of guilt for not having been able to assist in any rescue operation for them. She understood very well that there was nothing that the remaining crew could have done to help her husband and she went to see every one of them and consoled them too.

It eased their feeling of guilt and helplessness to hear her sober words and feel her understanding of their inner feelings.

Guttorm came to see Thorhilde at her home where she was sitting in silence with her grandmother and her two children, both of them were now very sick. Yngve looked to be ready to leave this world at any time and Thorgunn was also becoming severely sick now.

He knew that he was dealing with two very strong women of the highest character and integrity, and that his words were not all that necessary. He expressed his sympathy and said that a ceremony for the dead would be held at the church the next day, and that he hoped that they would come.

They sat together for a long time in silence and just felt the goodness that everyone in the room possessed, before the priest bade them farewell and left.

Chapter IV

The grieving wife and mother - 1327

The men, women and children of the Northwestern Settlement were all assembled at the church and Guttorm conducted a passionate sermon for the three dead sailors. He mentioned all their good qualities, their loyalties, their love for their families and for the Lord.

The atmosphere was very solemn, and the people though very touched by what had happened, were all very practical. They knew very well that life had to continue even in sorrow and the very difficult days to come.

Thorhilde stayed very calm during the sermon and ventured home with Gyda right away afterward to avoid being seen as weak.

She and her grandmother were sitting together for a long time in silence before Gyda finally spoke, "Is there anything that I can do for you, my little Sunshine?"

"Yes there is! May I cry out on your shoulder?"

She leaned herself toward her grandmother and put her head into her old and fragile shoulder and poured her heart out with her tears. They were sitting like that for a long time before Thorhilde pulled herself together and said, "Grandmother, I feel better now, and we need to have something to eat."

The farm that she and Gyda occupied was one of the oldest farms in the Northwestern Settlement and was managed by a younger brother of Gyda, who lived on a neighboring farm. He saw to the animals and the harvest and haying. As compensation, he was to have what they did not need for himself and his large family, and eventually inherit the farm.

Gyda came from a large family, and she was the oldest of twelve children, many of her siblings were still alive and supportive to her and Thorhilde.

They were all very family-oriented with strong bonds between generations and siblings, as well as cousins.

Thorhilde put out the food, which had been provided for them by her grandmother's younger brother and they ate in silence, after having said grace.

"I am worried for my children, grandmother!" Thorhilde said in a solemn and still voice. "Neither of them are fairing well. Do you think the Lord will take them away from me, grandmother?"

"You know, Sunshine, there is a saying that some children are too good for this world! This may be the case for both Yngve and Thorgunn! When you look into their little eyes, it's like seeing into the eyes of angels. They are so pure and so innocent."

"Maybe you are right, grandmother. I have been preparing myself for the worst."

Later on that night after she has seen to the children, she walked down to the fjord and sat herself on the bank.

She was in a melancholy mood and gazed out toward the vast amount of water, when suddenly, she started sobbing uncontrollably. She buried her head in her hands and tried in vain to control herself. After a long time in solitude, she looked out at the fjord and shouted loudly, "You stole my father away from me. Was that not sufficient for you. Why did you have to steal my husband from me too? What have I done to annoy you so much?"

Then, she broke down completely again and started shouting the names of her father and her husband loudly, "Please, you cruel and merciless sea, bring them back to me, I need them here! I am so lonely."

After a while, she started pleading with the Lord, "Please, Lord, I know that my father and my husband have left me in this life. I'm afraid that my two precious little children are leaving me too. But, please let me be with them in the next life, and please give me the strength and courage that I need."

Over the next few days, she returned often to the bank of the fjord and sat there in solemn silence, grieving her fate upon this very earth that she has been born into. Sometimes, she cannot stop herself from sobbing and even crying out loudly the names of her husband and her father.

A few of her neighbors noticed it and told Gyda.

One evening, her grandmother came down to the fjord and sat with her. She brought a shawl with her to cover Thorhilde's shoulders.

"We all have had times in our lives when deep sorrows seem to be overshadowing our lives, my little Sunshine. I have had mine, and most other people have had theirs."

"At this point, I am most concerned with my own!" Thorhilde answers her sharply, but immediately regrets her harsh words. "Please forgive me, grandmother, for being rude toward you!"

"That is OK. But, be a good girl now and follow me back to the house, and please do not come back here anymore. A few people around here have already taken notice of you and they might think that you are loosing control of your mind. You must let go of your husband, and your father!"

Thorhilde, being the wise woman that she is, understood that it was her concern for her that was behind her grandmothers admonishment, and followed her quietly back to the house.

After entering the house, she said to Gyda "Grandmother, I am very tired. Will you please see to the children for me? I need to sleep!"

"Of course I will, Sunshine. See you again tomorrow!"

The next day, they were all summoned to a meeting at the church by Guttorm. Even though it was a house of the Lord, it was also a place where important announcements were given. Guttorm were standing together with the survivors of the journey to Bergen. There were seven of them, and they were all looking very sad and serious. The leader of the sailors began, "I have been selected by my fellow survivors to tell you about our voyage,

"Our ship left the Northwestern Settlement in early spring in order to be back before the fall storms. We had good wind and sailed directly to Bergen without any stops at all.

"When we arrived, we immediately approached a merchant whom we knew well and who has traded with us for years. He received us joyfully and did everything that could possibly be done to accommodate us. We were even invited to stay with him. But only half of the crew would stay in his quarters at a time, the rest would stay on board and guard the ship and cargo. There were always many loose elements hovering around the ships for easy money.

"He told us that King Haakon V Magnusson had moved the Norwegian capital from Bergen to Oslo.

"When we asked why he had done so, he explained that before Haakon became King of Norway, he was the heir to the throne and was made the Duke of Oslo. Probably because he became accustomed to living in that part of Norway, he began to slowly move everything from Bergen to Oslo.

"When we asked him if that change had made any difference for the people in Bergen, he told us, 'Of course, it makes a big difference! Bergen is no longer the most important city in Norway. For us merchants, it means a big loss in trade. I suppose that for the islands in the west, including Greenland, it will be a catastrophe!'

"How come? We asked."

He replied, "You must know that after Greenland and Iceland became part of Norway, the King imposed a royal trade monopoly on those islands. That may have worked to a degree, if the King would have followed through to make sure that it was implemented."

"You said that it would only work to a degree, but, what does that mean?"

"A free trade is always the best for all parties involved. However, when someone tries to monopolize or direct the trading, even with the best of intentions, it will become more expensive to ship merchandise. Inevitably, a monopoly will need to have a control function with often highly paid overseers, and that is expensive.

"Before, we were able to trade freely without any royal control, and you and other nations could also trade freely, and we all would benefit from it.

"Also, what is really sad is that by moving the capital of the kingdom out of Bergen, the sea and our alliances to the west are not that critical any more. The situation became even worse, when the King's only daughter, Ingeborg, who was heir to the throne of Norway, married the Swedish Duke Eric of Soedermanland.

"Their son, Magnus Eriksson, then became the king of Norway in 1319, about eight years ago. This new King has established very close connections with Sweden, Denmark, Wendland and Germany.

"And believe me," he said grimly, these alliances will lead to the downfall of our country."

"It sounds really sad!" we said. "Is there anything that can be done about it?"

"Probably not. However, there is even more bad news for both of us, for us, who are merchants of Bergen, and for you, who are living on the islands far away to the west."

"What is the bad news that could make things even worse?"

"Way back in 1250, King Haakon Haakonson made a trade agreement with the Wendish city of Lubeck basically to secure Norway with the grain they would need, and they were to be paid in dried and salted cod, lutefisk."

"What was so dangerous about that?!"

"Seemingly nothing, but for anyone who has followed the rise of Lubeck and Rostock on the Wendich coastline there are big warning signs. The merchants in Lubeck and Rostock have taken the lead in forming a society of merchants, which stretches throughout central Europe and even has established connections with Russia and Africa."

"But, isn't that good for all of us?"

"No, it is not good for all of us. It is only good for some of us!"

"How come?"

"For example, this society of merchants are now trading aggressively with Russia and they can get walrus tusk, meat, seal hides and polar bears furs much cheaper than any price we can offer, but the transport route is much shorter.

"They are also transporting elephant tusks from Africa, which has made the price of walrus tusks fall dramatically.

"Another thing to your disadvantage is that the ships from Lubeck would be far superior to your ships in an armed confrontation. Their ships are much larger, especially taller, and are built with a fore castle and an after castle."

"So, our ships would have virtually no chance against them in an armed conflict? Why doesn't Norway build a navy like that to so that we wold be able to defend ourselves?"

"Neither the King nor any of his counselors are interested in the navy. They are merely more involved in inner Scandinavian intrigues, making deals with Sweden and Denmark, in which Norway is bound to be taken advantage of."

"Why would that happen?"

"The Norwegian High Nobility, which could have backed up Norwegian interest has become almost extinct in their male lineages. This will lead to male foreigners marrying with the females of these formerly proud families and they will take control of their assets and positions."

"Is there nothing that could be done to stop this? Why couldn't the female heirs marry Norwegians?"

"Good question. But, the nobility would never marry under their stand.

"One thing more of concern, the Wendish cities of Lubeck and Rostock are also in league with the big bankers in Europe, especially the Italians. They can raise mighty military forces, armies and navies to have it their way."

"So what are you going to do in order to protect your interests?"

"We're going to leave the country for Liverpool, Bristol and Dublin, perhaps even for Amsterdam."

"Are you really serious about this?!"

"Yes we are, and I would advise you to also seek out the new land to the west of you, the that you have visited so many times. I have had word of the situation in Greenland and I don't think that you have a future there anymore. It also seems that the weather is becoming increasingly colder and colder every year.

"Here, in Norway, we have become almost totally dependent upon grain from Lubeck, and soon they will have us in their hand. You will be totally dependent upon a Royal Monopoly for grain, and trust me, my friends, neither the King's heart nor his adviser's hearts are with you.

"They only took an interest in Greenland when there seemed to be something to be exploited from the island."

"So, what about you here in Bergen?" one of us asked daringly. Have you also lost interest in us?"

"We run our trade as a business, and I am somewhat ashamed to tell you that we will only trade with you if we can make a profit on it. I will be realistic with you. Today, your walrus tusks, meat and hides or whatever you might bring here will be traded at such a low price that it will hardly be worth your voyage."

"That is really straight talk!"

"One thing more, when, and not if, the Wendish league of traders take over here in Bergen, I can assure you that they will not be interested in the Atlantic trade. It is far too dangerous for their ships, which are not built to withstand such stormy oceans. Furthermore, there will not be enough of a profit in it."

"I can tell you, here and now, that none of us told him of our plans to migrate to the land to our south, even though he said that it was a good idea.

'Finally, the Bergen merchant asked us, 'What can I do for you, my friends? It might be the last time that I will be able to do anything for you!?'

"We need tools of all kinds, weapons and seeds of all kinds, as well as flour. Can you assist us in that? We will pay you with what we have on board which is our usual cargo."

"I will trade with you, even if I don't profit from it. My ancestors have traded with Greenland for centuries. Tomorrow, I will go aboard and inspect your cargo."

"The next day, he generously gave us the merchandise that we needed and we left Bergen in mid July.

"On our journey home we docked at the usual harbors for safety. First, in Lerwick in the Shetland Islands. Then, in Thorshavn In the Faeroes Islands. Lastly, we docked for several days in Reykjavik in Iceland and waited for better weather reports.

"The weather reports were not favorable for the area to the west but fall was coming and we could not wait any longer. As we sailed west, the weather became windy, but we managed to enter the East Greenland stream and we hoped that the stream would bring us safely past the southern headland of Greenland. Unfortunately, as we approached the turning point, a freakish wind suddenly blew toward us and the rest you know already.

"We received all the help that the people of the Southeastern Settlement could give us. They asked us to convey their condolences to the families who had lost one of their loved ones.

"We brought all the cargo that we took on board in Bergen, it is now all unloaded.

After that report, all the men, women and children went back to their own homes filled with their own thoughts about the news, and filled with deep empathy for those who had lost their husbands, fathers, brothers and sons to the brutal and cruel sea around the southern part of Greenland.

As the days went into the late fall in the year 1327, it was obvious to everyone at the Northwestern Settlement that the weather had changed. The winters were coming earlier and earlier and they seemed to be lasting longer and longer. Some people even measured the glaciers in the inner fjord valleys, and they were slowly becoming larger, inch by inch.

Thorhilde was not so much worried about the climate of Greenland. She now knew that her destiny was not here in this settlement, but further south.

Also, both of her children had been sickly for a long time and they had become weakened by their illness. She often wondered how much longer they would live.

She thought to herself that the time that we have left together should be joyful, so that we can all cherish the memories we created together. She asked her grandmother to help her teach her children the old songs which the Norwegian mothers used to sing to their babies.

Thorhilde gathered the four of them in a little circle on the floor and Gyda taught them the old children's songs of Norway. Instead of feeling the utter despair that had earlier filled the room where the children were sick, the room now became filled with smiles, songs and laughter. It was so pleasant for all of them to be there.

Her little boy, Yngve, had his whole face full of smiles and a sweet happy look in his eyes. He stretched his small arms out toward his mother and wanted to come and sit closer to her. She held the little boy in her arms close to her body to keep him warm. He was so tiny and had lost almost half of his body weight during his illness.

Generally, the Vikings never took their children into bed with them, but Thorhilde felt that tonight might be the last time that they would ever have together, and that they should be together. "Be cautious that you might sleep on them and choke them," Gyda warned her sternly. "It is not advisable to do that. Too many children have been killed that way. If it happens, it is even punishable by law."

"They are older now, and I take my chances, grandmother!" Thorhilde answered. "I will be very careful, and I will do it only for this one night."

"So what do you think will happen tomorrow night? The children will cry to come into bed with you again!"

Thorhilde brought them both into her bed and held them close to her while she prayed to The Lord for them. She also softly sang one of the old Norwegian songs that her grandmother had taught her.

Because she was both a wise and a cautious mother, when the children were sound asleep, she carried them very gently over to their own beds and went back silently to her own. She again prayed for their protection and well being, even though she knew in her heart that they were not going to live much longer.

The next morning when she met Gyda, who was already up, she said smilingly, "I followed your advice and put them back in their own beds when they fell asleep. Both of them were so peaceful and so happy. Come, let us go and see them."

Yngve greeted them with his usual broad and happy smile on his face, but when they tried to feed him, at first he wouldn't have it, then he threw it up on his little pillow. When they offered him some more, he looked up at them scared and waived his arms in protest.

"I don't think we should try to force him to eat, grandmother. He maybe dying. Let him die as a happy child."

They fed Thorgunn, who was also sick. Then, they turned back to Yngve. He tried to smile at them in a way as if he wanted to convey a message to them. "He is ready to leave us!" Thorhilde said with tears in her eyes.

They watched in sorrow as his little and frail body fought and lost the battle with his disease, and that early afternoon his spirit left his little earthly shelter. He leaned back and seemed to be in complete peace.

Thorhilde sank down by his bed, but could not control herself anymore.

Later on, Guttorm and some of the neighbors came to condole her and asked if they could be of any help. Thorhilde asked for a quick burial, and they agreed on the next afternoon.

"Please let me be alone with my dead child tonight. But, please bring the small coffin in here so we can dress him and let us bury him tomorrow afternoon."

Thorhilde and Gyda changed everything on him and washed him. After that, they put on his best clothing and put him gently into the little coffin. Gyda also helped her with Thorgunn and asked if she should stay with her during the night.

"Thank you, grandmother, for all your concern, but please let me be alone with my son tonight."

After Gyda had left, she dressed herself for the night and knelt down by the little child, who had now become cold. She thanked the Lord for having allowed her to have such a beautiful child in her home for more than three years. "Dear Lord," she prayed, "please let me have him for eternity when my time comes to return to you."

Then she quoted from the book of Job, "The Lord hath given and the Lord hath taken away. Blessed be the name of the Lord."

The next morning Gyda found her asleep on the floor next to the coffin. "Arise, Thorhilde, and get dressed. Soon the priest and our neighbors will come. Yngve looks very beautiful."

They waited for the priest and the neighbors to come.

"Do you want to take a last look at him before we close the lid?" Gyda's younger brother asked. "Of course," Guttorm said with a stern voice, but with full of sympathy toward Thorhilde.

Thorhilde stepped toward the coffin, but when she saw Yngve laying there so peacefully and even now with a smile on his mouth, her feet suddenly gave way under her, as she fainted and fell to the floor. Gyda said, "Take the child to the cemetery and let me take care of her. Wait with the ceremony until we come along."

They all watched the little coffin being lowered into the cold Greenland soil. Thorhilde had now taken control of herself and thanked all the people who had come to support her and give their condolences.

Sadly, her little girl, Thorgunn, only lived two more weeks before she also died.

Now Thorhilde had no more tears to share, and she watched in stunned silence as Gyda and her friends and neighbors conducted everything that needed to be done.

Being a childless widow from a good family, Thorhilde was now becoming an attractive object for marriage. However, she made it quite clear to her grandmother and Guttorm that she had no plans for marriage in the near future.

As the days went by, she had many thoughts in her head, and she struggled a lot within herself about her future. The answer to that question came on a clear sunlit day.

Guttorm, the Parish Priest, and a delegation of elderly men came to her home and asked if they could come in. When they were all inside,

Guttorm said in a solemn and quiet voice, "We have decided that you are to become our Queen and the leader of this settlement before we leave the next spring or summer for the land to the south."

Thorhilde was overtaken with the utmost surprise and could only say, "Why me?!"

Gyda was sitting next to her and did not look surprised at all. She said to Thorhilde, "Do you remember that you promised me that you would undertake anything of importance that you would be asked to do in the future?"

"I do remember that! How long have you known about this, grandmother?"

"For some time. You are the best choice."

Thorhilde asked the men, "Why have you chosen me to be your Queen and leader, instead of so many capable men?"

One of the elderly men stepped forward and said, "For many reasons!"

"Name some of them!"

"You are of noble lineage in legal marriages to the King of Norway, the High King of Ireland, and to the Clan Chiefs of both Clan MacDonald and Clan MacLeod.

"There are no close family ties to the largest families here, so we are not concerned about any favoritism.

"You are both wise and insightful, and in good health as well. Furthermore, you have experienced sickness and sorrow. You are well thought of by everyone and you can control yourself. Beside that, everybody in this settlement seems to like you, or even adore you. Will you say, yes?"

Thorhilde looked at Gyda for a moment and confidently smiles,

"My answer is, Yes!"

Chapter V

The crowning of Thorhilde - 1328

It was early March in the Northwestern Settlement and the air was still moist and cold, as if the winter would not let go. The settlers had been very busy during the winter months in complying with the directions given them by Thorhilde.

As she was to become their Queen, she was to lead and counsel. She knew very well that many of the settlers were very independently minded and they also did not like to be bossed by anyone.

She had resolved to always counsel with all the heads of the families before making any serious decisions, and then to even ask them for a unanimous acceptance. Any mistrust or feelings of belittlement were to be avoided at all times.

Her grandmother, Gyda, had advised her to treat everyone with the utmost respect and courtesy, in order to receive the same in return. "Remember," she told Thorhilde, "that all true Vikings consider every free man, as well as woman, equal to him or herself, and strongly denounce the newly created aristocracy, both Royal Family, as well as Ecclesiastical."

When she had conducted her first counsel session with the heads of all the households in the Northwestern Settlement in the late fall of last year, she didn't feel nervous at all. A great calm had come over her as she came to understand that it was her prophetic destiny to act in this important office that she had been chosen to fulfill.

Her grandmother had also counseled her to treat men and women equally. "The women of our Northwestern Settlement are just as strong-minded and capable as the men are. Always remember that!" she admonished Thorhilde.

"Also, remember that the boys and girls that have grown up here under such harsh and lonely circumstances are fully matured at a very young age, probably around the age of twelve. Do not ever think of considering them like children."

The first thing that Thorhilde put on her agenda was combat training. She knew very well that they would be on their own in the new continent and they may sometimes be surrounded by hostile natives.

She asked the men and the few women who were present what they thought of putting combat training so high on the list, and they were all positive about the necessity of such training. Then, she proposed, "Since we are so few in numbers we will also need to train and arm our women and children!"

The men and women present thought this proposal over for a while and then, they all nodded in agreement.

"At what age shall we start to combat train and arm our children?" one man asked.

"What age do you think?" Thorhilde replied calmly.

The men and women present debated it quietly for a few minutes and then asked Thorhilde to make the decision for them.

"I think that all children of the age of six years old should carry a knife, both for a tool and also as a weapon of defense. They must be taught by their parents how to use it as a tool, and taught to only use it as a weapon in order to defend themselves when their lives are in danger.

"Furthermore, from the age of nine years old, all children shall carry a short sword and they must also be trained to use that short sword in combat by the men most experienced in sword combat that we have in this Northwestern Settlement."

Everyone present was stunned, but they had all already consented to her decision.

She also continued, "Also, I want all adults as well as children to be trained in archery."

"We do not have many bows, and not many men among us who are trained in archery," one of the men objected.

"Then, we will start today by making bows and arrows, and start the training in how to use them start immediately. We have the whole winter in front of us to master it. We will take the material we need, from whatever place we can find it."

After they all went home, the household leaders who had been summoned as counselors were in awe because of Thorhilde's firm and direct leadership style. They admired her for her strength and wisdom.

As the winter months went by, the tasks that she had asked them to implement had all been well taken care of. She was proud to see how well they all cooperated, and how well they mastered the use of weapons.

She hated violence from the bottom of her heart, but was so wise and so smart that she knew that her main responsibility was now to see that they would all be safe in their new homes in the new land that they were going to settle.

She knew their strengths and their weaknesses well.

Many of them were immensely independent and very capable to doing almost anything they were asked to do. From their childhood, they were used to working on the farm and assisting their parents in all the necessary duties of operating a farm. Many of them had also been on hunting expeditions and were also experienced in traveling on the great river systems of the vast continent to the south and west of Greenland. They were totally reliable in everything that they were entrusted to undertake.

Many of them were also experienced sailors, as well as capable of building and maintaining their small ships.

As a weakness, she would count their somewhat rebellious nature. She understood well that in order for the settlers to survive, she would need to spend a lot of time arbitrating between disputing families. Being together on a small ship for days and weeks, could become a problem.

There were some one hundred farms altogether in the Northwestern Settlement. Some had but a few family members living there, while others consisted of large extended families living and working together on the same farmstead. Altogether, there were some one thousand and eight hundred people living there.

They were all together and ready to leave, except for an elderly couple living on one of the outlaying farms.

"We have lived here all our days, and for the few years that we have left to live, we prefer to stay here in our own home."

Thorhilde didn't argue with them, but asked for their solemn word of honor that they would not tell anyone coming to the Northwestern Settlement looking for them where they had gone.

"Of course we won't!" they both promised.

"We probably only have but a few years left to live. God be with you when you leave!"

The men had been testing all of the small ships that were built. They were pleased that the ships both sailed and rowed well, but were not built sturdy enough for the treacherous waters in the southern headland of Greenland.

As cargo was also to be carried on board the ships, the decks had been strengthened.

Thorhilde had been given their coming migration, as well as their settlements in the new land to the south and west a lot of thought, and she knew that she would have to discuss these matters with her council of household family heads.

While she was walking around in the settlement, she visited every single one of the farms and talked to their whole families. She knew every single one of them and tried her best to admonish, encourage and counsel them all.

The beauty of their settlement area was astonishing. It was a world made for heroes, not for cowards and weaklings. There were glaciers, fjords, mountains, green pastures, domestic cattle and wild animals. In the fjords there were whales, seals, cod, salmon, eider ducks and a variety of other fish and birds all ready to be harvested.

But what she loved most were the people who lived in the Northwestern Settlement. They were the hardiest and toughest people to be found anywhere on this earth. Hardly any complaints were ever made regardless of what sorrows or problems would befall them.

When she thought of all the injustices of the Norwegian aristocracy, and the wrongdoings of even the church toward them, she became infuriated with anger within herself.

How could they belittle such hard working and proud people and bring them from free men and women down to mere tenants and virtually serfdom? It was beyond her comprehension to understand how they could reduce these men and women with their proud and free ancestry like this.

"But now we are going to leave our serfdom for a land of liberty" she said to herself.

Her grandmother, Gyda, was not fairing well at all and Thorhilde was worried about her. She often wondered how much longer she would be with her. One day, Gyda told her that she had asked for the Lord's permission to live long enough to see her granddaughter become crowned as the Queen.

The early spring counsel in March was convened and as they all came together one of the men asked her a direct question, "When shall we officially crown you as our Queen?"

"When we are ready" Thorhilde answered.

"When is that? I don't think that we should delay it any longer! Let us plan for it today! Who is in favor?"

Everybody shouted, "Yes, we are in favor!"

They talked, counseled and laughed together for an hour before they agreed on the crowning ceremony to take place on the first Sunday in May. "We are going to make you a crown of gold and some beautiful clothes for the ceremony," one of the women said.

"You will also need a personal guard!" one of the men shouted.

"Not here in the Northwestern Settlement, I hope?" Thorhilde answered.

"Of course not, but you will need a personal guard in the new land, and they will need to be trained."

"Choose six men from the foremost of the equals to guard you as our Queen and leader!" shouted one man and the rest shouted with joy.

"There is a need for educating everyone in the Northwestern Settlement," Gyda told Thorhilde. "Ignorance is as dangerous as idleness, and if not watched out for, it will eventually become worse and worse and even destroy us as a civilized people."

"Could that really happen to us?" Thorhilde asked in great surprise.

"There is always a danger to that, Sunshine. When we as a people are living in a land of plenty, idleness will become our most dangerous enemy, along with ignorance. We must be very much aware of these two enemies. A too comfortable society, a society where we don't have to struggle for survival, can become a way of slowly dragging us down into idleness first, and then soon after ignorance as well. This would lead us to become a lazy, ignorant and idolatrous people."

"But that sounds horrible, grandma!" Thorhilde almost cannot believe her own ears.

"You probably have heard the saying that idleness is the root of all evil. That is a very, very true saying and we must be on our guard to avoid falling into the trap of coziness and laziness. Both the Greek and Roman civilizations were destroyed because of it. Furthermore, we Greenland Vikings must never take slaves as they did of old. That will drive us into a dependency on other people's work and lead us to becoming prideful and lazy. We must never become dependent upon free or even cheap labor either. Exploiting cheap labor is not much better than becoming dependent upon slavery. Either of them would eventually lead us toward destruction."

"But we are an enlightened people, grandmother. How could this really happen to us?"

"Do not feel too sure about that, Sunshine. It could happen to us if we do not watch out."

"But we will be watching out! I promise you that, grandmother."

"I strongly admonish you that as long as you are our leader, that you keep your people busy. There are so many things that we may learn from the world around us, both from the ancient world, as well as from the current world. Learning from our life experiences is what builds strong and independent communities."

"That I understand, grandmother. What do you want me to do about it?"

"First of all, I admonish you strongly to visit all families of the Northwestern Settlement and see to it that they know the commandments of the Lord, and also see to it that they are implementing the Lord's commandments in their lives."

"But isn't that Guttorm, the Priests job?"

"Not really. He cannot do that alone. Being a good man and even a priest is not sufficient to exercise such authority. Both he and his young successor are very good people but the people of the Northwestern Settlement are looking to you for leadership and direction. The settlers know Guttorm well, but he is now getting old and it will take time for everyone to become known to his young successor. It might even take twenty years for Guttorm's successor to build up the trust and confidence that is necessary for him to lead, even in spiritual matters.

You, my granddaughter, are the one who the settlers will look up to and come to for advice – far more than any clergy."

"I am amazed, grandmother!"

"You ought to be amazed. It will place a large responsibility upon your still young shoulders!"

"I hope that I will be up to the responsibilities that have been given me and that I do not betray the trust which everyone, including the Lord, has given me!"

"Sunshine, you are the most qualified person for this position in the whole of the Northwestern Settlement."

"Please, send a ship to Iceland also, and purchase all the copies of the Nordic Sagas that have been written there by Snorre Sturlasson. Times are bad in Iceland now and you should be able to find merchandise here to trade for the papers and books that they have available."

"Why is it that we would find such important papers in Iceland, but not in Norway, grandmother?"

"The Icelandic people have always been the best read people in our part of the world, and maybe in the whole of the world. Even though they are very well read, many of them are now starving to death."

"But, doesn't the King of Norway assist them? He has a trade monopoly with Iceland. Doesn't that mean that he, in return, has some responsibility toward them?"

"The king of Norway is so occupied with inner Scandinavian intrigues, that he does not find time for us nor the starving Icelanders."

"May we take some of them with us to the new world?"

"Good question, we should admonish as many as possible of our own families first to come here. But, be very careful not to tell anyone in Iceland about our plans. The King of Norway and the Archbishop of Nidaros have long ears."

"We must also bring with us to the new world the spirit of learning that is so deeply rooted in the soil and heart of the Icelandic people."

"I totally agree with that, grandmother."

"The spirit of adventure is still with us, but don't take it for granted. It will be our companion forever, unless we feed it."

"How do we feed the spirit of adventure, grandmother?" Thorhilde asks.

"We implement it into our lives, Sunshine!"

"How do we do that, grandmother?" Thorhilde asks.

"We explore the world around us as much as we can, and never stop exploring!"

"I am overwhelmed by your wisdom, grandmother."

"Thank you, Sunshine!"

"Remember to always feed the three spirits of Learning, Adventure and Labor."

"But are not learning and adventure the same, grandmother?"

"No, they are distinctly different. To learn is to experience things, while adventure is to dare doing things that others are too frightened to do. To be adventurous could be both seeking out new worlds as well as trying out new devices."

"In considering the first spirit to be fed, how do you propose to deal with that, Sunshine?"

"We will start with the learning and the reciting of the commandments of the Lord. However, I do not think that it will be necessary for the settlers to learn Latin. It ought to be enough that the two of us and the priests have a command of that language."

"Very good, Thorhilde, please continue."

"I also think that the settlers should be able to read the copies of the Icelandic Sagas, and I propose that we start classes early this fall in order to make good progress on that learning."

"Good, Thorhilde!"

"We should also learn more about making iron from nature, as they did in Norway of old. There must be a few people in Iceland that could teach us how to do it. We also need to become more proficient in blacksmithing, so that we will be able to make our own tools and weapons, especially plows and swords."

"Why don't you act immediately, Sunshine, and send for some people from Iceland who have all of this knowledge. Of course, ask them to bring their families as well. They must be willing to join us in our migration."

"We must arm and teach everyone in our Northwestern Settlement who is capable of bearing arms how to use them. We will also need to train them in combat strategies and tactics. I will bring this up in the next council with the heads of the households in order to hear what they think about it."

"Have you anything more to say about learning?"

"Nothing that I can think of now, grandmother, but something might come to me later. There are always many things to be learned."

"What about the necessity of Labor, Sunshine? In our settlement, everyone is already occupied with something. If the people weren't working, what do you think that they would be up to?"

"They would be up to nothing good grandmother, except if they were studying or learning skills."

"Sunshine, educate and train our settlers, but also keep them busy at all cost. Encourage them to try to invent or improve our hunting weapons, our agricultural tools and any other useful domestic device. Improving our weaponry will turn out to be a necessary improvement for the defense of our settlements.

"Send out parties to explore as much of this vast continent as possible, both on ships and by canoes, as well as by horseback and on foot. Chart as much of the land as possible, for our own benefit and also for the benefit of those who will be coming after us.

"Try to learn and become familiar with the native languages of the closest natives, as well as the most widely spoken and important of the other languages. Get a working knowledge of them so that we may benefit from frequent oral interaction with the natives and become more friendly. Also, get a good knowledge of their customs, as well as their religious beliefs.

"Respect them for their skills and friendliness, but never take after their bad habits."

"I will teach my people to do that, grandmother!"

"Remember to constantly guard your smaller children, or they may become kidnapped and sold as slaves perhaps to places so far away as beyond the limits for a rescue party to reach them. If we are not alert, they may try to steal our cattle and weapons. Some may not see anything wrong in that practice.

Be alert all the time!"

"I fully understand that, grandmother!"

"You know, Sunshine, that anybody without a meaningful task in life will eventually fill their spare time with something that is not meaningful, or which could even become directly destructive. Be alert!"

"I will be, grandmother!"

"You probably know that the Norwegians are the most adventurous people on this very earth. How do you think they became like that?"

"Probably, it was because by their life circumstances!"

"Exactly, Sunshine, and also because of their origin, they were an enlightened and sturdy people who migrated to a land far to the north, where they had to learn to fight for survival."

"You told me that it was part of their prophetic destiny!"

"They were enlightened in a way that is quite obvious. Their law system is the most righteous in the whole world. They have been observing the Gulathing Law for at least the last seven hundred years, while other powerful people in Europe and elsewhere in the world that we know of were only having a sort of traditional law system, which greatly favored the rich."

"But, most of the rest of the Europeans are also Christians, grandmother!"

"True enough, but unfortunately the church have become more and more corrupted and together with a greedy, lazy and unrighteous aristocracy they were doing nothing but exploiting the common man and woman."

"It is good for us that we will get a new start, grandmother!"

"Do not overlook our opportunities, Sunshine!"

"You know, Sunshine, that the Norwegians explored the seas. They sailed through the Mediterranean Sea and the Black Sea, as well as far south along the West Coast of Africa.

After circumnavigating Scotland and England, they founded two large cities in Ireland, namely Dublin and Waterford. They settled the Isle of Man and the Channel Islands, and also made settlements in Normandy.

"Those were great accomplishments, grandmother!"

"Yes, they were, Sunshine."

The Norwegian King, Magnus Barefoot, managed to conquer all the islands to the west of Scotland, as well as the peninsula of Kintyre. He brought the peninsula of Kintyre into Norway by making a deal with the King of Scotland, whereby whatever he could steer his keel around should belong to Norway. Then, he had his men drag his ship across the narrow strip of land that bound Kintyre to the mainland while he was sitting at the steering oar."

"Is it still Norwegian?"

"No, King Malcolm of Scotland thought it was unfair that the Inner Hebrides should belong to Norway and proposed to purchase them. The Norwegian King, Haakon Haakonsson, rejected his proposal."

"Good for him!"

"Then the mainland Scots started to raid and plunder the Inner Hebrides and the clan chiefs of the Inner Hebrides requested assistance from the King of Norway. King Haakon Haakonsson mobilized a fleet of one hundred and twenty ships and sailed west to negotiate with King Malcolm of Scotland out of a position and show of strength.

However, King Malcolm of Scotland outsmarted him. He delayed the negotiations long enough for a fall storm to scatter the Norwegian fleet, and when the Norwegian King was left with a smaller force to guard him, the Scots attacked him and overpowered them in the battle of Largs.

"Oh, what happened to the Norwegian King? Did he get hurt?"

"The battle was indecisive, but due to late fall storms, the King's fleet pulled back to the Orkneys for the winter."

"The fleet stayed there over the winter. The clan chiefs of the Inner Hebrides admonished Haakon Haakonsson to return with his fleet and take Glasgow. He was also approached by the Irish Nobility who appointed him High King of Ireland and requested his help to throw the English out of Ireland. Unfortunately, Haakon Haakonsson became seriously ill during the winter and died in Kirkwall in the Orkneys. His men then returned home to Bergen where he was buried."

"How sad, was he a good king?"

"He was, Sunshine, and it was a tragedy for Norway that he should die so young.

Norwegians also explored and settled Orkneys, Shetland, Faeroes and the Northern part of Scotland as well as large parts of west Scotland."

"That seemed to be a large landmass!"

"It was, and we were superior at sea."

"But, are we still superior at sea, grandmother?"

"No, we are no longer the superior nation at sea. Other nations have modernized and armed their ships much better than ours. You heard what the men were told in Bergen!"

"It was a sad story to hear, grandmother."

"Yes, it was, but so is life sometimes. Ships from the Southeastern Settlement sailed on the Eastern Coast of the great continent to the west of us and founded several colonies on the coast there. Also they founded support settlements on strategic places on the Iroquois River Water system, some by the river itself and some on an island by the mouth of the ocean."

"Do we have we any contact with those people now, grandmother?"

"Unfortunately, we in the Northwestern Settlement have lost all contact with them over the years. I do hope that the Southern Settlement have kept in touch with them."

The settlement is now preparing for the crowning ceremony and everyone both young and old are excited.

The magnificent Crown, as well as clothing fit for a Queen are already in place, and they are all exited and waiting for the last of the new ships to come back from Markland.

This time, the ship had a much longer voyage than usual due to the voyage they made right into the land of the Cree and the Assiniboine.

The ice was just melted enough for the crew to sail the rivers and Lake Winnipeg and to return in time. To the surprise of the settlers, they saw two native men on board the ship. The sailors present them as the Cree Chief and the Assiniboine Chief, who they had been persuaded to come along to watch the crowning ceremony.

Thorhilde knew of this beforehand, and had approved generous gifts for the tribes to support it.

Being the insightful leader that she was, she fully understood the importance of good public relations.

"I also want the two native chiefs to teach our people a working knowledge of their language, as well as their customs. Also, what things will trigger anger or frustration among their tribes, and what things will trigger happiness and peace."

Thorhilde made it clear to everyone that she expected them to treat the natives as their equals, also to learn as much as possible from them in every way possible.

She also clearly understood that they would report back to their tribes on our strengths and our weaknesses, so she ordered a display of arms, and had them watch a mock combat of highly skilled Vikings.

She also demonstrated the most skilled archers in action, as well as the ships fully mounted with warriors. She also supervised it in a way intended not to scare them, but rather to impress them.

She could see that they watched these demonstrations in deep thought.

The Cree Chief had asked for some weapons as a gift, and the Assiniboine Chief had asked for some mares as a token of friendship between the settlers and their nations. To the dislike of some of the settlers, Thorhilde agreed to these gifts.

"If you want to please the natives with gifts of weaponry and horses, you better give them your own property, not ours," they told her angrily.

"We will solve this problem," she answered smilingly. "I will send a ship to Iceland to purchase the weapons and horses that we need for the gift and I will pay for it with merchandise from my own property. I will also see to it that it is done quickly."

"Who are you going to send?" the men were still unhappy with her generosity toward the two natives.

"If necessary, I will go myself" she answered calmly. "But, I would prefer volunteers. Who wants to volunteer for a quick trip to Iceland for me?"

Fortunately, enough loyal men stepped forward and volunteered, and she told them, "Leave as soon as you are ready. You can trade my animals for the horses. Furthermore, you can use all of the gold and silver that I have inherited to trade for the weapons. I want a good relationship with the Cree and Assiniboine Nations."

She was very calm about the whole thing, and understood well that if she was not cautious, it could develop into a big problem.

The angry men calmed down and one of them approached her with a sorry look in his face.

"We didn't want to offend you Thorhilde, but we know these people. They are sly and untrustworthy. Please do not let them fool you!"

"They live after other laws than we do. I want a good working relationship with them, and I am well aware that they may not be as well educated or skilled as we are, but we will treat them as equals to us, in order to honor our deeply rooted Viking traditions as well as our inherited Christian traditions."

"You are quite sure about this?" the man asked her.

"Yes, I am sure of that," Thorhilde answered the man smilingly.

The time for the crowning ceremony had come and they were all summoned to a meeting place close to the parish church.

Some of the women of the Northwestern Settlement had dressed Thorhilde in a beautiful blue and white robe, combat style. It was decorated with silver and pearls and was really very gorgeous looking.

On her head, she was wearing a Viking helmet with a gold cross on the front of it. She was girded on her left loin with a beautifully decorated belt holding a medium size highly decorated sword. Her shoulders were adorned with flowers and she was carrying a round and beautifully decorated shield in Scythian style.

The crown was waiting for the ceremony by resting on a purple pillow.

Guttorm and his assistant were dressed in their best priestly clothes and all of the settlers were wearing their Sunday clothes too.

Before the actual ceremony was to start, Guttorm wanted to make a short speech. He had it well prepared and was now ready to deliver it.

He started, "Beloved fellow settlers in Christ, I am so happy to see this day come to us. It is a day that I have waited and longed for for a long time. We all know why this had to come to pass. It was actually impossible to avoid it.

"This day is a glorious day for all of us, but it is also frightening for some of us at the same time.

"Both I and my assistant would probably be burned alive at the stake for administering witchcraft or sorcery to you, if we were caught by men sent out by the King of Norway. They would gladly do it on behalf of the Church.

"Both Thorhilde,who will now become our Queen, and her grandmother, Gyda, who is such a close adviser to her, would probably be put to the sword if they were caught by the King of Norway.

"And for the rest of you, certain imprisonment. You would be lucky to have your life spared, but there would be a sure return to serfdom and misery. Consequently, we have all chosen freedom and adventure, instead of serfdom and drudgery.

"We all know that we are to enter the shore of a vast continent that is mostly unexplored, at least inland, even though some of us have been there many times earlier.

"I, here and now, ask for the Lord to protect you, both on your voyages as well as your travels in the new land. May He always be with you and protect you during your voyage and after you have settled too!

"Let us start the ceremony!"

Thorhilde was guided forward by the priest to an ornamented chair, which was especially decorated for this occasion, and she was seated in it.

The assistant priest gently removed her Viking helmet and gave it to one of the women assigned to assist in the ceremony. Another woman also assigned to assist, gently removed the hairpins that she had used to fasten her hair under the helmet. Now, her waist long, beautiful red blonde hair was flowing freely down her body.

She was a sight for Gods as she sat there and everyone present was stunned with admiration for her majestic beauty, as well as the grandeur of the setting.

Guttorm took a horn filled with holy consecrated oil and poured some of it gently directly unto her skull, after having parted some of the hair gently.

He first looked toward heaven, then toward the people and lastly toward Thorhilde and declared, "Thorhilde Arnfinnsdaughter, having authority from God and his only true church, I anoint you the Queen of the Northwestern Settlement of Greenland, as well as all affiliated settlements in the new land to the south and west. I bless you with prosperity and wisdom and God and his holy angels shall be with you until your mission in this life is over. Amen!"

One of the women came forward and dried the residue of oil from the top of her head.

Guttorm was given the pillow with the golden crown.

He took the crown and lifted it up high so that everyone could see it and declared again, "Thorhilde Arnfinnsdaughter, with authority from God and from the settlers of the Northwestern Settlement of Greenland, I crown you the Queen of the Northwestern Settlement of Greenland and all affiliated settlements in the new land to the south and west of us. Amen!"

He then placed the crown on Thorhilde's head.

The crown was made of plated gold by experienced hands and was decorated with beautiful stones and pearls. It is as resplendent as any crown to be seen anywhere in the world.

Everyone present was feeling the holiness and peace that was then resting upon everyone present. The impact that it has on them was tremendous. They all looked happy and are full of life.

If the king of Norway had happened to learn about this crowning of a Queen ceremony, he would have sent a fleet of warriors against them, and they would have been trapped inside the narrow fjords with nowhere to escape. They would be surrounded by glaciers and high mountains that formed a barrier to the north, the east and the south.

Nevertheless, the decision had been made and now it was time to act.

After the crowning ceremony, Thorhilde returned home exhausted, removed her royal dress and went to bed for awhile.

After awakening, she met with Gyda and they both sat for a long time in solemn silence together. Both of them felt like they were in complete spiritual harmony with one another.

Gyda broke the silence and said, "Now, I have fulfilled my destiny on this Earth and will be permitted to leave and go to my ancestors."

"Grandmother, do not talk like that!"

"Sunshine, we have experienced some wonderful years together. Cherish them in you heart. We will meet again in the next life."

Thorhilde started to cry. "Please, do not leave me yet grandmother!"

"I will still be around for a while, Sunshine. Come let us have something to eat and be happy for the remaining time that we have together!"

All settlers of the Northwestern Settlement were summoned to meet together and made an oath of allegiance to their newly crowned Queen.

That event was as solemn and holy as the anointing and crowning event, which was probably because everyone eight years old and older was participating in the ceremony.

Thorhilde was again dressed in her full royal regalia with the beautiful crown on her head. Her shield and helmet were slung over her shoulder and a sword girded on her loins.

Guttorm and his assistant, as well as her bodyguard of six very capable young men were standing by her.

He asked everyone to come forward, one by one, family by family in order to kneel in front of her and kiss her hand. Then, they recited the oath of allegiance, family by family. "I hereby renounce all former allegiances that I have had to the King of Norway and to the Archdiocese of Nidaros, and promise solemnly to honor and obey the anointed and crowned Queen Thorhilde Arnfinnsdaughter of the Northwestern Settlement of Greenland."

They all participated wholeheartedly and they were unified in being happy. Thorhilde now understood in her heart that she would have their complete support, as long as they were treated fairly.

She also knew very well that they had a free and rebellious nature and was well aware that they would not take any nonsense from anyone.

Chapter VI

The migration to the south and west – 1328

Gyda called Thorhilde to her and wanted to talk to her, "Sunshine, now that you are the Queen of this free Northwestern Settlement of Greenland, I want to give you some further advice before I leave this world."

"Oh, not again grandmother! You know that I lost my husband and both my parents early, and that I only had my two small children with me for a very limited time. Please, don't you leave me also!"

"My little girl, I do hope to be able to strain my fatigued body to its outmost so that I can come with you to the Winnipeg Settlement, and be of some mental support to you."

"Thank you, grandmother," Thorhilde shouted with joy.

"I also want so much to have a peek into the land of freedom before I go to my ancestors."

"You will come with me in my ship, grandmother!"

"Thank you, I knew that you would offer me that privilege."

"But, grandmother, you have called me here for a specific reason, to give me some needed advice. What is on your heart?"

"I wanted to give you a stern word of warning, my love. You know that we have been robbed by the royalties in Norway, as well as by the church there for centuries. They have issued unrighteous taxes of all kinds, and the most recent tax they issued was an export tax for our merchandise which is to be sold in Norway, as if we weren't exploited enough beforehand."

"But, that is horrible, grandmother!"

"When we migrate to the new land, there will be dangers there too, but in a different way. The natives do not have the commandments of the Lord and they won't see stealing as being wrong, as long as it will benefit them."

"Is that really true, grandmother!"

"Unfortunately, yes, my dear girl. We must guard our animals, food and weapons all the time. Especially, we must guard our little children. They might be taken and traded with other tribes as slaves."

"This is really scary grandmother! How can we prevent that from happening?"

"We must always be on our guard, Sunshine!"

"Please, let me also give you another stern warning, Sunshine. Most of the natives are friendly, but we should not take after their idle ways. It might even become sort of contagious to you too. It will slowly destroy us as an industrious and reliable people, if you let that happen to us."

"But, how would that happen to us, grandmother?" Thorhilde said. "Now, we are so strong and trustworthy!"

"Remember the old saying, 'Idleness is the root of all evil.' The rot may start within our people as well if we are not careful to dig it out immediately. Here in the Northwestern Settlement, we have to work all around the clock in order to survive. Now, we are migrating to a land of plenty, but believe me, there will be dangers in that too."

"How could having good and easy living become dangerous, grandmother? I cannot fully understand that!" Thorhilde asked in surprise.

'You are only used to hard times, dear, and for sure you will come to experience the dangers of idleness and laziness in this new land. It could breed more and more rot and disrespect for what is good and right.

"By the way, Sunshine, how many trips have you been contemplating that we will need to make this summer? The ships are so small that we will need to make several trips altogether."

"Of course, I have considered the number of our people, the weight of our cargo and cattle which we could safely carry in one journey!"

"Remember, Sunshine, that when your forefather, Eric the Red, came over with the first large group of settlers from Iceland, only half of the ships made it ashore in Greenland. The rest of the ships sank with everybody on board, probably in the very dangerous waters to the south of Greenland.

"The only people who seem to have mastered those treacherous waters are those who sailed for the merchants in Bergen. Those ships were often crewed with sailors from both of the two Greenland settlements, who knew about the dangers and how to avoid them.

"However, the time when the merchants of Bergen were trading with us annually seems to be over. Our merchandise is no longer profitable to them."

"But that is not very loyal of them, grandmother. What about all the profit that they have made from us throughout the centuries?"

"Life was really good for us here in Greenland the first half of the three hundred years that we have been here."

"You have told me about that time, grandmother."

"So again, Sunshine, tell me how many trips you are planning for this summer."

"Four trips, grandmother, with the first trip in early May. We must plant the seed in our Winnipeg Settlement as soon as possible. I have planned for the heaviest items to be carried on board my ships since they are the largest and sturdiest of our little fleet."

The fleet was of some 20 small ships, as well as Thorhilde's ship, which was built as a warship, and was decorated with a fearful dragon head by the fore stem, as well as having a higher gunwale than the rest of the ships. Her ship was equipped with sixteen pair of oars as well as a magnificent large and colorful sail. The shields belonging to the warriors were hanging on the gunwale, and added to the splendor of the ship.

It was meant to both impress and to frighten any opponents. There was ample room for cargo and one hundred armed warriors, as well as some one hundred passengers.

The smaller ships were suited to carry a normal household of some sixteen people on average, including their animals, with their farm equipment and household goods. A ship fully loaded with everything needed, people and animals would be sunk down in the water almost to its lower gunwale, with a free board of only half a foot.

Obviously, sailing across with ships that heavily loaded could become very dangerous. To make the crossing safe, everything had to be in working order and the sea and the wind had to be favorable.

They had enough experienced sailors to crew the smaller ships with at least two men of sea and sailing experience on board every one of the twenty smaller ships.

The most experienced sailors cautioned Thorhilde to plan for the ships sailing at least two weeks on their passage from the Northwestern Settlement to the mouth of the Winnipeg River.

They advised Thorhilde to let the first group of twenty small ships with some four hundred men, women and children leave around the tenth of May, which would enable them to arrive at the southern part of Lake Winnipeg around the thirty first of May. Later on, they would arrive at their final destination by the junction of the Assiniboine River and the southern part of the Winnipeg River, probably around the fifth of June.

Before anything else, the settlers were to secure their settlements. After that had been taken care of, they would then sow their seeds. They would have with them all the seeds as well as some of the oxen, plows and agricultural tools needed for that purpose, and would have to get it done as quickly as possible.

Thorhilde's ship, called the "Dragon of Greenland" was to stay there for two months to guard the infant settlement. Then, it would return in late July, but now without every one of its one hundred warriors. The rest of them would be left to guard and assist the settlers.

The "Dragon of Greenland" would then return to the Northwestern Settlement and there supervise the migration and return to Winnipeg with the last group in late August.

Each of the groups would have with them two much smaller ships, without cargo on board, in order to assist in any eventual rescue emergency. They were former hunting and merchant ships.

Thorhilde ordered that all unmarried men between the age of eighteen and twenty-eight were to be considered as warriors. If needed, she could also call out any man, older than eighteen, as well as any unmarried woman older than eighteen but younger than twenty- eight years of age. Because this could become necessary, all of us must also be able and alert to defend ourselves against raids from neighboring native war parties.

Coming home tired and fatigued late one night, she was met by her smiling grandmother, "Come in and sit down and enjoy your favorite dish of lefse and lutefisk. We had better enjoy it while we can. We won't be able to catch cod in the rivers of our future home!"

"Do you really mean that we won't be able to have our favorite dishes in our new land?" Thorhilde asked in surprise.

"Remember, Sunshine, that we will be leaving one world and entering into another world. In the new land to the south and west, almost everything is different than where we live now."

"Tell me your thoughts about it, grandmother!" Thorhilde said with excitement in her voice. "That would be very interesting to me."

"There are so many things that will be different to us that it will take some time to describe them all, Sunshine"

"Please, take your time for that, grandmother!"

"First of all, our young ones will adapt fairly quickly, whereas our middle aged will take a much longer time to change the customs of their lives. Some of the very oldest of us will probably never adapt to the new circumstances at all. They will hang on to their old Norwegian ways of thinking and their old ways of doing things."

"Is there anything wrong with that, grandmother?

"Not really, but it will not be helpful either when we really need to adapt to the new world of ours."

"Grandmother, you have mentioned 'a new world' many times. Please explain what you mean by that!"

"Sunshine, absolutely everything will be different!"

"Tell me grandmother, I am exited!" Thorhilde shouted loudly.

"Well, first of all, the food is going to be different. Let us start with the grain that we use to bake bread. From Norway, we are used to wheat and barley. Even though we have brought seed with us, the time will come when we have to adapt to the grain that the native has cultivated and they call it maize."

"How does it taste, grandmother?"

"Somewhat sweeter and softer than our bread and not so nourishing either, but eventually you will have to become accustomed to it. Even to pronounce the name maize is difficult for us."

"Why don't we just call it the common Norwegian name for that grain which is Corn?"

"I like that name, Sunshine, we will settle for that. Then, we will be able to to bake Corn Bread for our families in the near future!"

"I have a feeling that it will be a delicious bread to eat, grandmother."

"The natives also have a food that they call yams that they eat as a side dish for their dinners. It is actually very tasty as well as nourishing. You better become accustomed to that as well."

"How interesting, grandmother, please continue!"

"The fish that you will catch in the rivers and lakes of the new world will be completely different from what you have been accustomed to from the fjords and the ocean around Greenland. Only the salmon and trout that you sometimes catch will be somewhat the same as you are used to now."

"What kind of fish can we expect to catch in the rivers and lakes of the new land?"

"They will be nourishing enough, but with a different look and taste."

"Will that really matter, grandmother?"

"Not really, but many of our people have strange eating habits and they are set in their ways. They might be fearful of their new foods, and they might not like the way they taste. Believe me, I know what most Norwegians are like."

"Will this land have a lot of wild fruits and berries that we are not accustomed to from Greenland?"

"Oh yes, Sunshine, there will be an abundance of blueberries, blackberries, currants of different kinds, as well as roots of all kinds. The blueberries we are used to from Norway compared to the blueberries that you are going to see in the new land are quite different. They grow on much larger bushes and the berries become much larger as well."

"Wonderful, I am already looking forward to tasting them! It seems to me that we are migrating to a beautiful land of promise, according to our prophetic destiny."

"Yes, Thorhilde. You have had a kind of vision."

"But, in addition to the food, grandmother, what else will we need to adapt to?"

"Well, the soil and grass are different from Greenland. It is far more difficult to till the ground than what we have been accustomed to. The labor of tilling and farming will take its toll on us. The flowers and trees are different from ours. We will need to learn, little by little, their names and their usefulness from the natives."

"What else?"

"Most of the wild animal life will be different. You will meet some very strange animals that most of you would not even expect did exist, except in your wildest dreams. Because of the warmer climate, there will be enormous amounts of insects which you will encounter, and they will astound you. Most of them are completely unknown in Greenland, and some of them are even mortally dangerous to man."

"How can little insects be so dangerous?"

"Sunshine, some of them, even if they are small, have very strong poison in them, so they are able to paralyze their victims and sometimes even kill their victims."

"Grandmother, you are frightening me!"

"Although it is rare that people get killed by them, there are rattlesnakes that can even harm the cattle! If you find that there are rattlesnakes where you have your domestic animals, you had better kill them all before they bite and poison the animals, or you."

"What are rattlesnakes, grandmother?"

"Rattlesnakes are very poisonous snakes that have rattles at their tale. They always sound their rattles before they strike their victims."

"Why would they do that, grandmother?"

"Probably to scare their victims, Sunshine. But, there is little need for us to fear them. They are fairly rare and you will get to know how to either avoid them or how to deal with them if you should encounter them."

"What else would be new to us, grand mother?"

"The climate there will be completing different from Greenland. Because Greenland is so close to large oceans, areas near its coastline will have an oceanic climate, which means that the climate will be affected by the sea temperature. Areas away from the coast in the new land will have a continental climate, which means that the climate will be much warmer in the summers, but with very cold winters."

"But, grandmother, we have already experienced some extremely cold winters here in Greenland!"

"Yes, even a continental winter that far north will be nothing to compared to the winters that we used to have in Greenland. On the prairie of the continent, some horribly cold winds will blow and you will need to tackle them in order to survive."

"I am sure that we will be able to, grandmother."

At last, the long awaited departure time for the settlers of the Free Northwestern Settlement of Greenland had arrived. It was early morning on the ninth of May, and all twenty small ships were fully loaded and ready to depart.

After an inspection, Thorhilde noticed that one of the ships has insufficient free board and asked the head of the household in charge of that ship, who was an elderly and stubborn man called Bjarni, to unload his oxen and load it on her larger ship.

He flatly denied that he did not have safe free board, and also claimed that he was the only one who could handle the animal properly.

Thorhilde considered his denial for a while, but realized that it would not be safe to give in to him. She said firmly, "Bjarni, I know that the animal belongs to you and that you are the head of this ship and crew, but you will be putting not only your own family at risk, but also our whole little fleet. I am not accepting your answer. Unload the oxen!"

"Has it gone to your head that you have been chosen Queen, your Majesty?" Bjarni answered sarcastically.

Thorhilde kept her calm and answered smilingly "I hope not, Bjarni, just unload the oxen. We will take good care of your oxen." The two sailors who were assigned to that ship listened in stunned silence and admiration. According to Viking custom, they were only advisers to the ship's captain.

The little fleet had received favorable weather reports for sailing the Davis Straits between Greenland and Helluland and they proceeded out of the protected fjords toward the open sea and freedom with everyone in a good mood.

On the deck of the "Dragon of Greenland," Gyda warned Thorhilde of an old saying, "Success will always bring you faked friends and true enemies. Watch out for Bjarni. He will not like you from now on. You belittled him in front of his whole household, as well as those two sailors."

"So, what should I have done? I have the responsibility for the rest of the fleet as well, including Bjarni's own family, and the two sailors on board his ship!"

"I know that, Sunshine. But, please be on your guard for him in the future."

"Certainly, I will, grandmother."

The ships formed a V formation with "The Dragon of Greenland" up in front and the two assisting ships sailing in the center of the little convoy, so that they could provide assistance as quickly as possible, if needed.

Each of the ships had been supplied with plenty of buckets and balers to be able to bale out any water that should come on board. Even a heavy rain was not very dangerous, because it actually could be baled out fairly easily. What was really dangerous was the freak winds and freak waves. They could destabilize a ship very quickly.

In May, it was too warm for icing to occur, even in the middle of the East Greenland Stream that streamed northward along the western coast of Greenland and then, after making a one hundred and eighty degree turn, proceeded southward along the eastern coast of Helluland, where it is called the Labrador Current. The fleet had to cross that stream twice.

For the first crossing of the northbound stream, they wanted daylight.

The only real danger with the crossing of the first northbound stream was that it often carried driftwood from as far away as Siberia, and that driftwood could even sink a ship if it rammed it hard enough.

The northbound current brought the little armada of ships a little further north before they had sailed across it. Then, using their compass, they continued sailing slowly straight west for two days. To be sure to be able to handle the more dangerous southbound ocean stream, they waited for the early morning light of the third day before entering into it.

The water and the air above it became colder immediately, and they saw that the stream was also carrying small icebergs that had broken off the large ice glaciers further north. They knew very well that they had to maneuver their ships across the stream, while avoiding the icebergs, before darkness came.

Due to decennia of arctic experience and good decisions by their sailors, the crossing of the southward stream was accomplished without encountering any problems.

Soon, they were in the strait between Helluland and Markland, and they saw landmarks that some of the adventurous settlers of Greenland were so familiar with. This was one of the areas that was always full of walruses, whose tusks had brought such prosperity to the Greenland settlements for decennia.

The elderly men remembered well those trips, and they enjoyed telling hunting stories to the younger ones, while pointing to places that they knew so well. Little did they know then, that sometime later, they would be sailing this area with their families and all their belongings, to seek freedom in the new world to the south and west.

The little fleet proceeded slowly. There was still ice floating in the water, so they needed to maneuver their ships with care.

Thorhilde was on deck enjoying the scenery that was now being displayed before her eyes. She saw the fleet of some twenty smaller ships sailing smoothly and majestically behind "The Dragon of Greenland." The air was crisp and clear and the environment surrounding them was nothing but fantastic.

The sea was full of life. There were seals, walruses and an abundance of polar birds all around them. "How may the Lord really have created such stunning beauty?" she said to herself in stunned amazement.

A Greenland whale surfaced close to her ship and the big whale seemed to enjoy becoming a part of the little convoy. Ever so often, it would blow up water and some of the spray even fell on deck. The whale even swam close enough to her ship to rub himself gently against the hull.

"It must be a male whale!" one of her sailors shouted. "He probably thinks that we are a female whale and is courting us!"

"Would he harm us?" Thorhilde ask in wonderment.

"No, but it may become annoying" the sailor answered.

Gyda laughed and exclaimed, "Now, you have even been courted by a Markland whale, Sunshine. Who might become your next courtship?"

"I will never become remarried, or even have a boyfriend, grandmother. I believe Erling and I were two people, who were only meant for each other."

"But, can you stand the solitude, Sunshine? It isn't easy to become widowed at such a young age. Nobody would blame you for taking a new husband."

"I feel that I can stand stronger alone, and my marriage shall be to the Free Northwestern Settlement of Greenland for the rest of my life."

"You are an idealistic woman, Sunshine, and I admire you for that. But remember, that there will be many days to come when you may feel the need of a true companion."

"Yes, I remember the saying that you told me, 'Success always brings fake friends and true enemies.'" Since I have become a queen now, many men will only want to marry me in order to become a Prince Consort."

"That is probably true, Sunshine."

Several days later, after sailing southwest across Hudson Bay, they arrived at the mouth of a fairly large river that the sailors told them would lead them to Lake Winnipeg. They also informed them that the Cree word Winnipeg means muddy. "It seems," Thorhilde quipped, "that we have sailed through both the Muddy Straight and the Muddy Bay and are now about to enter the Muddy River going up to the Muddy Lake.

In the river, the crew of the ships needed to take to their oars in order to propel their ships at a reasonable speed up river, against the current. The land around them was barren looking at first, but eventually looked more lush.

There was an abundance of beautiful flowers and moss all around them and since they were proceeding so quietly, they could also see an abundance of wildlife. They even saw polar bear mums with their cubs, as well as polar foxes and lots of caribou.

"We have an abundance of meat supply right here next to us!" one of the sailors told Thorhilde. "There is also an abundance of wild berries, as well as delicious wild roots to harvest from nature."

"This must be the land that God gave to Adam!" Thorhilde exclaimed. She is already in love with her new home.

After a couple of days traveling southward up river, they arrived at a large lake. "This must be Lake Winnipeg!" Thorhilde said to Gyda. "What a beauty!"

One of the experienced sailors approached Thorhilde and said, "On our starboard side, we will soon pass the estuary of the river Saskatchewan. That river would lead you northwest and further west, past some very fertile prairie before it reaches a massive mountain formation. We have explored it earlier and it is a fast running river that is not really suitable for us to navigate with our ships."

The fleet sailed further south through a narrower passage of the lake before it reached the southern part of Lake Winnipeg.

They made a short stop before they proceeded up the southern loop of the Winnipeg River. Experienced sailors and travelers told Thorhilde that this was the old traveling route over the Minnesota Prairie and further over the big lakes and the Iroquois River back to Greenland.

When they came to where the Assiniboine River met the southern loop of the Winnipeg River, Thorhilde decided that they should look for a good place to make a settlement. They anchored their ships and scouted the area for a good suitable site.

With skilled translators, Thorhilde had a lengthy conversation with the Assiniboine chief and asked for his permission to settle there for two years, before they would proceed further south to a settlement in Minnesota. He granted them permission.

All the ships unloaded their cargo of men, women, children, animals, storage and equipment before the whole fleet, except "The Dragon of Greenland," made ready for the return to Greenland.

In order to sail the returning fleet of twenty smaller ships, the settlers were asked to crew the ships with one extra man on each ship. This left each household short of manpower in establishing their new settlement. Furthermore, Thorhilde also ordered one of her warriors to sail on each returning ship. Compensation was made so that the eighty warriors who were left to protect the virgin settlement would also give a hand in all duties as they were needed.

Thorhilde had earlier counseled with the settlers that they needed to plant their seed and build fences to protect their plants and animals. After planting, they were to construct log houses, one house for each family with barns and cowsheds for the animals next to the house.

The settlement site that they had chosen was close to the river and was fertile with trees for both construction and firewood near by. It was also a good choice for a settlement that would need to protect itself from thieves, as well as guard against any attackers.

They watched the little fleet sail away northward and wished them good speed and good luck on their return journey, knowing that the ships were now much safer without any cargo on board. The sailors were so experienced that they could handle the ships across the lake and downstream the river to the big Muddy Bay with only two extra hands on board.

After the settlers had calmed down after their long journey, they were all exited about their temporary new homes.

The very first task that they accomplished was their stockade fences around their animals, because they did not want to lose them. Additional night guards were also set out to keep a constant look out for any intruders, either natives or wild animals.

Thorhilde also asked her warriors to be on watch constantly, especially for the children and the animals, the children first because the children were their love and their future, and the animals second because they needed them.

She also reminded everyone to sleep on their swords. "Be alert," she said, "even if the Assiniboine and Cree Chiefs have promised us friendship,.they may not control every individual man in their tribe."

After several days, they were ready to plant their seeds, and with the help of the oxen, they managed to break through the never-tilled soil of this tough land. Thorhilde was pleased to see how disciplined the men were. They were all pushing themselves to do their outmost. Every day showed an amazing improvement to the settlement.

One day in late June, they were awakened by joyous shouting from their guards, "Our ships have arrived and they are all well and sound!"

They all crowded to the shore in order to watch the little fleet arrive, being rowed steadily up the river toward the camp. It was a beauty to watch and Thorhilde could barely keep back her tears, because she was so thankful to the Lord for having brought them all here safely.

She knew that the waters between Greenland and Winnipeg Bay could soon become more treacherous, due to sudden changes in weather conditions and freak waves which could shove water into the little ships faster than they could bail it out. She also knew that the settlers would not, under any circumstances, discharge any of their cargo or animals into the ocean in order to get a higher free board. They were now free and independent men and would either sink or sail to their beloved destination.

The Greenland Stream that originated in the Siberian part of Russia often brought some large trees, which could easily sink a fully loaded little ship if they hit suddenly and hard enough. She also knew that that same stream that was turning south by Helluland could carry icebergs big enough to sink a ship.

Thorhilde had been praying almost constantly for their protection on that very dangerous trip. She felt consoled by the knowledge that Guttorm was coming along as the leader of that trip and that they also had some very experienced sailors with them on each of the twenty ships.

Their voyage had even taken a few days less than the first trip, due to warmer weather and longer daylight. The sun had warmly bathed them and they all said that their voyage had been as pleasant as could be.

Thankful to the Lord, they all knelt down together with Guttorm who offered a heartfelt prayer of thanks to Him who had kept them safe.

Guttorm also advised all of them to thank Thorhilde for her immaculate planning of the voyages.

She smiled when she heard their thanks, and knew in her heart that it was the Lord and her grandmother to thank for their safe voyage.

The little fleet quickly returned again to Greenland to bring the third party to them, and they all watched them sail down the river.

Soon, they all became busy in erecting their log houses for their families. They were also very happy to reunite with their friends and neighbors again in this their first settlement in this new land of theirs.

With Guttorm here, they decided that they should build a small church, so that they would have a place to meet together often, and hear the spoken word of God again, and be able to partake of the Holy Communion again.

In almost no time, the church was built and it was consecrated by Guttorm in a very solemn ceremony with all of the settlers attending. He consecrated the building as a holy and protected place for the settlers, and also as a place where they could come to partake of the holy sacraments, and also become closer to the Lord.

Even though the settlers were prone to look for signs and wonders, and a few were superstitious to a large degree, many were also very religiously inclined. In their hearts, they were really seeking to live the way that they knew is the way that the Lord wanted them to live.

Guttorm knew that, but he also knew of their rebellious nature and the need to balance between the practical events of every day, which would have its challenges and the very right way which the Lord was hoping for them all to follow.

Guttorm was a very highly respected man among the settlers and Thorhilde was very happy that he was there among them in order to back her up if a serious internal conflict should start up among them.

They were now all living much closer together than they were accustomed to and they had all been crammed together on small ships for a long time. Altogether, this was an unusual challenge for people who have been used to no one telling them anything about what they should do.

Seemingly, things were going well, but Thorhilde had a feeling that something was developing under the surface of things and she prayed constantly to the Lord for his guidance, so that she might be able to solve their inevitable internal differences.

Time went by quickly as they all worked hard to establish their new temporary settlement, until one day their third little fleet arrived. They were received with more joy and celebration among the settlers.

After they became settled in, "The Dragon of Greenland" was made ready for departure, together with the other twenty smaller ships in their little fleet.

Thorhilde left the eighty warriors in the settlement and only brought her six man guard, as well as six other volunteers to manage the large ship. She wanted it to have a large free board in order to transport the heavier cargo from the smaller ships. Late July had come and the last voyage would be made in late August when the first fall storms usually started.

Thorhilde bade them all farewell and asked for their steadfast cooperation in keeping the settlement safe and in bringing any internal conflicts to Guttorm, who would need to arbitrate them. He was a man of the Lord and also a very wise and experienced man she admonished them before leaving.

Gyda also bade her granddaughter farewell with tears in her eyes, "May the Lord be with you and protect you, my little darling," she exclaimed softly.

"Thank you, grandmother, and you had better stay well and alive until I return."

The fleet proceeded quickly down the river and was pushed into Lake Winnipeg, where they encountered their first problem. There was very little wind to fill their sails and they had to rely on their oars men. That method is reliable enough for moving forward, but is time consuming and very laborious.

Because of this slow speed, they cannot get back to the settlement before mid-September, when the fall storms will become more dangerous, she thinks to her self. She shares her concerns with one of the older and very experienced sailors and he tried to console her,

"At this speed, it will take us at least a week to reach the northern part of Lake Winnipeg, which will be a loss of some five days, compared to a normal voyage with prevailing winds, but the river will push us quickly down to the big bay that the Cree call the Muddy Bay or Winnipeg Bay in their language.

"Crossing of the bay might take us two weeks, at the worst, but with even some wind we could shorten it to ten days. By then, we will have lost some ten days altogether. In the straight south of Helluland, we will sail faster and not lose much time. Altogether, we may be half-a-month late getting back to the Winnipeg Settlement. I predict that we will there by mid-September."

Thorhilde understood that the sailor had decennia of experience with these waters, he had given her a very sober prediction of the possible outcome of their voyage.

It turned out that his predictions turned out to be very accurate and they sailed into the fjords of the Northwestern Settlement of Greenland in late August.

Thorhilde's heart leaped and she almost stumbled when she saw their precious settlement before her eyes. She knew that this would be the last time that she would ever see it. The farmhouses looked so lonely and desolate now, without the settlers and their animals around. She almost cried again, but she controlled herself.

The last party of settlers were almost ready for departure and the crews of the fleet stayed ashore for a few short days in order to rest and regain their strength for the final crossing.

Thorhilde visited the elderly couple who had refused to leave and she asked them kindly if they had changed their minds about staying.

Both of them flatly refused to leave, and Thorhilde knew them both well enough to not try to change their minds. She gracefully wished them well on their remaining lives.

The old woman said to her, "Here we have lived and toiled all our lives, and here we are going to die. Do not be afraid, because we will not give out any information about your whereabouts to anyone. Within a year or so, both of us will probably be gone to our forefathers. May God bless you and your little party of travelers on your voyage. But, watch out for freak winds, and for the revenge of Bjarni. He will have it in for you at his earliest opportunity!"

"I will be watchful, and may the Lord bless you too, both of you!"

The fleet of ships loaded quickly and "The Dragon of Greenland" took on board so many of the larger animals that there was only a three quarter foot free board.

There was freak wind on the ocean now and the old sailor warned Thorhilde, "We will need to have plenty of bailers ready because we will surely take in water. I recommend a speedy crossing of the ocean until we are south of Helluland.

"But, don't we need to cross the streams in daylight?" Thorhilde asked.

"Of course" the man answered. "Leave things to me, and try not to worry. We are going to be safe."

The next morning, they encountered not only the dangerous northbound Greenland Stream, but also a powerful north wind blowing straight into the stream, which created freak waves, which soon showered the ships with seawater.

The leading sailor shouted, "Let us make a fast crossing of the stream, full sails and everyone to the bailers."

"Will we have icing?" one of the men asked.

"It is not cold enough yet. Had we been here just two weeks later, then we might have encountered ice"

"So, we can call ourselves lucky?"

"Yes, you can!" the sailor replied.

For a while, it was looking very dangerous as the wind increased and the waves poured onto the heavily loaded ships. "Have the animals lay down!" the man shouted again, "we are already beyond the center of the stream and the conditions will soon improve."

One of the smaller ships was in obvious trouble and both of the two support ships were maneuvering closer to it. The smaller of the support ships, a former hunting ship, managed to come alongside on the windward side and thereby provided some protection for it from the freak waves.

After sailing safely through the northerly stream, they were now beyond the most dangerous part of the voyage, even though the wind was still building up from the north.

The fleet fought the fierce wind for two more days before they entered into the southbound stream flowing close to Helluland. This southbound stream was also quite dangerous because the northerly winds had increased and were now creating larger ocean waves, which might quickly become very dangerous to the smaller ships.

Late in the afternoon, they sailed safely to the south of Helluland, where they are all gave thanks to the Lord for saving them all from the winds, the waves, the icebergs and all the other floating objects in the streams.

Ships, people and animals have all taken a severe beating by the forces of nature, but they are all in a mood to persevere as they navigate the strait between Helluland and Markland. The Northerly still hauls around them, but they are sheltered from the waves of the ocean.

Thorhilde almost frowned with the thought of them being only one day later to cross, and she acknowledges that they have been protected by higher powers.

The crossing of the big bay leading onto the northward Winnipeg River does not take long with such a strong northerly wind behind them. The sails of a couple of the smaller ships were severely damaged, but they still managed to stay within the fleet.

By the tenth of September, they entered the river and even though they were somewhat protected from the wind behind them, it was still enough to propel them fairly quickly into Lake Winnipeg. The elderly sailor warned Thorhilde, "This lake can sometimes be as dangerous as the streams of the ocean because of the wind, which is blowing as fiercely as it is now. We must proceed carefully and be aware of large trees floating in the water. Those trees are as capable of sinking our ships as fast as anything that we may encounter in the ocean between here and Greenland. I strongly advise you to only sail with reduced sails and only in broad daylight and even then, with extreme caution."

Thorhilde understood well the wisdom given to her by this experienced sailor and quickly ordered that his advice was to be followed precisely.

Soon, they all saw the wisdom of his advice. They saw the evidence of the rampage of the strong north wind. The wind had uprooted several large trees, which were now floating low and almost unseen in the water.

With the Lord's benevolence, as earlier predicted, the battered ships, crew and animals of the last voyage safely arrived at the Winnipeg Settlement around mid-September.

Chapter VII

The Winnipeg Settlement and internal conflicts- 1328 -1330

Gyda was so happy to see Thorhilde again and was almost in her tears when she embraced her."It took you so long to come back darling granddaughter. I have been so worried for you."

"We encountered the first fall storm but with help from the Lord and experienced sailors we made it through safely. I am so happy to see you again grandmother!" Thorhilde exclaims joyfully.

"How are things going in the settlement grandmother?"

"Not to well Sunshine. There has been a lot of backbiting and contention among the settlers."

"Can not anything be done about it?"

"It will be difficult to mend. A lot of harm has already been done to the settlement. Hopefully we will be able to solve it together. "Tell me what have happened!"

"The men are questioning the wisdom in coming here as well as the wisdom in making you the queen of the settlement."

"What caused this questioning, grandmother?"

"A lot of the problems are centered on Bjarni and his extended family. They have now used their spare time to spread nasty rumors about you and your extended family as well as on Guttorm and his assistant."

"Grandmother, I must attend to this immediately. Do you think that I should try to speak to Bjarni and his family?"

"Please do not try to do so Sunshine! He so hardened in his decision to dislike you that it will only make things worse. I will advise you to call a Viking Thing that act like a court and where we can settle grievances between us. The Thing has the authority to pass judgment and finally settle any disagreement. It will take place outside and in daylight, as well as in full publicity. Ask for a vote of confidence from them all. Ask them who not will support you to leave the settlement the next spring with all their belongings and a fair amount of ships if they are many!"

Thorhilde asks for Guttorms advice on the matter and he tells her that he is aware of the problem and fully supports her. "We cannot let this tear our settlement and future apart!" He tells her with passion in his voice.

The Viking Thing is summoned and Guttorm is to be the speaker. He begins as follows "Dear friends, brothers and sisters in Christ, it has come to my knowledge that a lot of backbiting and contention has sprung up among you. This is not the way that we have been brought up to in our former beloved Free Northwestern Settlement of Greenland. It has also come to my attention that many of you are questioning the authority of Thorhilde our appointed Queen.

Let me remind you again of the circumstances which led to her election. For many years I struggled with my oaths to both the Archbishop of Nidaros and to the King of Norway. I saw the injustice that they poured out upon us settlers, and especially upon us in the Northwestern Settlement of Greenland. After many sleepless nights and lots of prayers I decided upon us leaving for this choice land and to become free men and women again loosened from the yoke of unjust taxations and unjust rule. Furthermore I advised you to choose a King or a Queen as a leader, and you all choose Thorhilde to be your Queen. You all gave your oath to her and promised to support her."

Guttorm continues "You all know that giving your word in an oath is a very important decision. If you break your oath you will be dishonored"

"So why did you break your oat to the Archbishop of Nidaros and to the King of Norway?" Bjarni is interrupting him in a loud and angry voice.

"I had no choice, but to act the way I did. The Sovereigns that we submit ourselves under and sustain with our oaths are also to protect our lives, freedom and property. Have they done that for us?"

The men became all silent. They knew that he spoke the truth.

"So why did we have to bend down and kiss her hand. She is just like one of us." Many of the men laughed.

"That part of the ceremony was instigated by me, to make it beautiful and sacred. I am sorry if you felt it otherwise."

Bjarni ask to speak to the Thing. He says "For centuries we have lived as free men on Greenland. Even though we have our oaths to both the Archbishop of Nidaros as well as to the King of Norway, we were enjoying our lives as free men with both the king and the archbishop far away from us. I propose that we the Thing dethrone Thorhilde and release her of her duties. We now longer need a Queen to reign over us. Let us have a show of hands of all in support of that motion!"

The people at the Thing are stunned with surprise. Not many had expected him to be that outspoken.

Thorhilde looked around and saw a few hands in support, mostly from his own family, but none from her own guard and not even one from her one hundred warriors, even though one of them, Olaf, was a very son of Bjarni. It made her heart swell with warmth and thanks, and she knew immediately that she was in both command and control of the situation.

She addressed the Thing and said "A proposal has been made and it is of such a magnitude that I think that we shall let everyone here counsel their families and ponder it until tomorrow. I propose that we do so and also that we shall first of all tomorrow have Guttorm read us the Viking Law and tell you of the consequences that will follow if you want to carry out your proposal.

"So what consequences might there be of it?" Bjarne asked stubbornly.

"One that comes into my mind immediately is that you will become dis-fellowshipped from the rest of us and will have to leave this camp immediately. Of course we will help you to dismantle your homes, stables and cowsheds and re erect them some miles further away from us. But if you choose to take that action against me, Guttorm and the majority of the Thing you shall also take the full consequence of your choice and start packing. I however do hope that you come to your senses and refrain from doing so. Gladly I will forgive you of your insulting words and do also hopes that you can forgive me of any harsh and insulting words from me to you. What do you say, Bjarni?"

Bjarni seems to calm down from his rage and says tauntingly: So you are sorry for what your Royal Highness?"

The Thing is stunned in silence.

Thorhilde smiles warmly and answer s him "I think it eats you that I ordered the oxen discharged from your ship due to a low freeboard. I had no other choice, but to do so. You wouldn't listen to reason."

"That is not the reason!" Bjarni knows that he is caught in childish behavior and wants out of if with his manly honor intact.

"So what is the reason Bjarni?" Thorhilde asks softly.

"We now longer need a Queen to reign over us. You have done your job for us."

"Why don't we let the Thing decide that tomorrow Bjarni?" Thorhilde answers kindly.

The families walk home slowly and in complete silence. They all know that Bjarni is wrong. But many of them fear him because of his temperament. He has already intimidated quite a few of them. He is not a wise man but he is a strong man and a good talker and also clever and sly.

Coming home Thorhilde is met by Gyda that greets her with those words "You acted like a true Queen Sunshine. The Thing will tomorrow turn him down, but be aware of him. What you said about the ordering to discharge the oxen from his ship didn't make it easier for him. Now he is foaming to get to you."

"Is it that bad grandmother?"

"Yes it is Sunshine; you have hurt his manly pride. Have your guard close to you in your future."

"Even at the Thing grandmother?"

"Yes Thorhilde darling, even at the Thing!"

"But isn't everyone at the thing to be unarmed according to Viking Law grandmother!"

"Yes they are Sunshine, but devious people may not follow the law, and if they are up to mischief and they know that every one but themselves are unarmed, it will be a good time for them to strike."

"What shall I do grandmother?"

"From now on always have your guard with you wherever you go, and tomorrow at the Thing pack the one hundred warriors around you, and tell them to not let anyone come close to you."

"If there is a conspiracy to take your life, they will strike tomorrow."

"Why do you think so grandmother?"

"Bjarni is bound to get the Thing against him. He might have intimidated and fooled a few to follow him, but without him there is no leader of any capacity to go against you again."

"So what do you propose grandmother?"

"We will first have Guttorm read the law and let those that want to address the Thing do so. Then Bjarni will propose the vote of dethroning you. He will loose and he knows that, but he hopes to have as many as possible of the men with him. I beg of you Sunshine to not hold anything against those that will support him. They have been fooled and intimidated by him. Right now he is doing his flattering, if necessary and intimidation if that suits his purpose better. You just keep your calm and have your guards around you."

"When everyone is done speaking what do you propose that I do. Everyone is looking for me for leadership grandmother!"

"Propose that the Thing make him "Varg i Veum" meaning outlawed. Anyone may kill him unpunished."

"Isn't that a harsh decision grandmother? After all he has a family to take care of."

"True, but he has always been a very difficult man to deal with and now when we are all in a very vulnerable situation, he has decided to act. If you out of kindness let him stay with us, he will become a constant problem to us. He is a master of intrigues and you will have to deploy guards around you always and may never let him to close to you or ever turn your back on him.'

"You are probably right grandmother. But first let tomorrow come."

"One thing more darling, I know very well some of the warriors. I will ask them to stay back from the Thing as far as the law allowss and have their weapons ready for a surprise attack."

"How come, that you know so much grandmother?"

"Sunshine, my grand mother told me many stories of how royalties were dethroned. Nothing seems to be to low for anyone that wants to dethrone a king or a queen. It goes from intrigues to flattering and purchasing of enemy support to stabbing, suffocating and direct warfare."

"Where any of our ancestors killed that way grandmother?"

"Unfortunately yes, becoming a queen or a king means that you sometimes have to make decisions that are not pleasing to everyone."

The next day dawns, cloudy and cold, and they are all, but the armed warriors in reserve, at the Thing.

Thorhilde is surrounded by her guard and the warriors who have all left their weapon behind as far away as the Viking law require them to do.

Guttorm first stands, and in a solemn voice he reads the Viking Law to them. After that he says "After what happened yesterday. I want everyone above the age of twelve to come forward and renew the oath to our Queen. I feel that this oath of honor have to be recited to steady our minds. Choose again today who you will follow, Thorhilde our rightly elected Queen who we already promised to sustain with a solemn oath of honor, is asking for your sustaining vote once again today!"

Having finished reading the law, he asks if anyone wants to come forward to speak.

Bjarni stands up and says "I have been pondering the proposal of Thorhilde all night and I am not comfortable with her. I propose to the thing that we dethrone her! Who is in support of me?"

Only half a dozen men step's forward and Bjarni looks around with anger in his face as if he had hoped for more people to support him.

Then Thorhilde rises and says "I am very sad that it should come to this Bjarni. Now I will propose for the Thing that they make you "Varg i Veum" and outlaw you from our fellowship altogether. "Who in this Thing is in favor of the outlawing of Bjarni Thorvaldsson?"

More than half of the Thing steps forward immediately and soon after almost all of the rest follow suit.

Thorhilde speaks again "I will propose for the Thing to dis-fellowship the three families that are supporting Bjarni Thorvaldsson and to have them move some miles away from us and stay there during the winter to come. But by the end on the month of May the next year they must move far away from our settlement. Where you go will then be to your own discretion. You may travel south on the big rivers, east towards the big lakes or return north again towards either Greenland or follow the cold steam southward along the eastern coastline of this big continent.

You shall be entitled to take Bjarni Thorvaldsson as well as three small ships but not any of the hunting or trading ships. Also we will assist you in moving your homes, stables, cow- and work sheds to your winter quarter. Who is in favor of this proposal?"

Before it comes to a vote, one of her faithful followers steps forward and asks "Why are you so lenient to these people. They have been intriguing against you for months, and last night they very even discussing to move against you in open rebellion with weapons in their hands?"

Thorhilde knows that this faithful man is only concerned about her safety and answers him "We are Christians and are living a higher law than these families that obviously have left the spirit of the faith. I know that they are dangerous but do feel that we will be safe enough staying close together for the coming winter. These three families that I propose to have dis-fellowshipped all have families even some of them are small children. I feel no need for revenge against them"

"They might be plotting with the natives against us." Another of her follower admonished her.

"We have a very good relationship with both the Assiniboine and Cree Nations, and I do not fear an attack from them. They have both been with us for months."

"Bjarni is creepy enough to promise them our horses, cattle and weapons if they go in an alliance with him" a third man says and continue "I propose to the Thing that we put Bjarni to the sword and fine the rest of them. Let them stay with us so that we can monitor their behavior. That will keep us safe."

Thorhilde understood immediately that the last proposal to the Thing was the best for their common safety. Even though she did not like to propose a death sentence on anyone, she knew that the Thing had an authority higher than Kings and Queens.

Thorhilde then replies "It has been proposed for the Thing that Bjarni Thorvaldsson shall be put to the sword for his rebellion against our Viking Law and that those who have been fooled and intimidated by him shall stay with us but be fined for their transgression. Step forwards everyone that is in favor!"

Almost immediately everyone but the three families steps forward.

"Seize him and put him to the sword immediately!" Thorhilde commanded.

Bjarni wakes as almost from a trance and started to swing a short sword that he had hidden under his cloths. "Whoever comes near me shall have a taste of this he shouts." He was a stocky built man with a barrel size chest, and had immense physical strength in him. Half a dozen men of normal strength were no match for him. Also his ferocious temper would scare any opponents.

The men form a circle around him and grabs whatsoever might be used as a weapon for protection.

Bjarni knows that he is doomed but shouts with a glowing fury in his eyes "Before I die I shall take at least some of you weaklings with me."

Quietly one of the men manages to come close to him from behind and lock his arms and disarm him. His hands get bound behind his back and a block of wood is placed before him.

Guttorm comes forward and asks "Bjarni, do you want to confess your sins before you go to your ancestors?"

Bjarni is as proud and stubborn as ever and answers "The only thing that I regret is that I didn't manage to dethrone your Queen and to take the lead of this settlement myself."

"Do you want to take farewell to your family before you die?" Guttorm asks again.

"My own son Olaf has turned against me and I will never ever more have anything to do with him. For my wife and the rest of my children and grandchildren I bid farewell."

"Then let us go forward with the execution." Guttorm tells the men in charge.

Before the execution can take place, Ragnhilde his wife rushes forward screaming and throws herself at the feet of Thorhilde and says "Please my Queen, give him "Grid", meaning pardoning him. You as our sovereign have the power to do that. Use this power now, please, I beg you?"

Thorhilde now faces the most difficult decision of her lifetime. She is virtually holding a life in her hands. She knows the consequence of a Grid. Bjarni will be around, full of hatred, and ready for trouble. She pulls herself together and replies "Motion denied, Carry on with the execution!"

Bjarni kneels down and put his head on the wooden block, and within seconds his head is severed from the rest of his body.

As is common for the burial of criminals in Norway, he is buried outside of the consecrated burial site. His own family is watching in stunned silence.

His own son Olaf is not even shedding a tear. He knows well that his father got what he deserved. What he does not tell anyone is that his father came to him in disguise the last night and asked him to murder Thorhilde and Gyda in their sleep and that he would then propose him Olaf to be the most suitable man to lead the settlers in the future.

If Bjarni had hoped for this, he was miscalculating his own son. Olaf became so disgusted with his own father that he only hoped that a death sentence would be given by the Thing.

The Thing then fines Bjarni's supporting families of all their horses to be given to the crown. They all looked battered, humiliated and vengeful, but at the same time considering themselves lucky to be alive and still in fellowship with the rest of the settlers.

Fall went by and winter came suddenly to the settlement. Now the settlers for their first time were to experience a continental winter. Luckily there were plenty of trees to burn close by, and they kept their fires going constantly.

Thorhilde remembered what Gyda had admonished her to do. "Never have your people become idle. That will only breed later problems."

She had a lengthily conversation with Gyda of how to make the winter become a time of progress and to avoid idleness and superstition. Gyda tells Thorhilde that the settlers are prone to seek answers to their questions, by turning to ancient superstition, rather than asking the Lord. As an example she tells of an event that she knows happened recently in the settlement. As an answer to the question about the harvest the coming year, the participants spread some grain on the floor and let a couple of hens start picking. If the hens start picking in the middle, the next harvest will be good, but if the hens start picking around the perimeters, the harvest will be poor. I fear that the settlers are moving themselves further and further away from the true source of counsel. So why not make it a season of learning, and thereby try to counteract superstition and heresy?" Gyda proposed.

"How interesting grandmother, what subject do you propose that we start with?"

"We should start with the most spoken language of this region. There are three large and important tribes on the northern plains.

The Assiniboines as they are called by their neighbors, or the Nakota Siouxs as they call themselves, are the most northern tribes of the Sioux Nations.

Further south of where we are now, are the hunting grounds of the Dakota Sioux tribe. They are living on the upper Mississippi River and The Minnesota River water systems. Most likely they are not going to welcome us when we get into their tribal areas in a couple of years. Then southwest of us where we are now and to the west of the Dakota Sioux tribe is the third of the Sioux tribes, the Lakota Sioux tribe, also called the Teton Sioux by their neighbors. They are a very warlike tribe and are a constant danger to our brothers the Mandan Nation. The three very powerful Sioux tribes are all parts of the Sioux Nation and they are all Siouan speaking. I propose that we invite our friends the Assiniboine and Cree Chiefs over and ask if they can supply us with teachers of their language as well as guides for our further travels in the continent. Probably they cannot vouch for a safe travel among the Dakota Sioux tribe. They do not like any strangers on their territory. We must be very careful when we are on the upper Mississippi.

One day, the tribal Chiefs of the Assiniboine and Cree arrived at their camp followed by a large group of warriors with their families along as well.

Thorhilde put on her crowning dress and received them with a courtesy fit for a Queen. They were too many to fit inside her large longhouse which were built the same way as the Norwegian longhouses, and could house a fair amount of people, but they were so many that some of them had to be placed outside near to the door. She had the man that was most aquatinted with their language to come and be their interpreter. After a lot of formalities were over Thorhilde invited them all to stay with them for some time and to partake of their hospitality. The Native Chiefs accepted the invitation but soon made it clear that they were there in another matter.

They wanted horses and weapons as tokens of an everlasting friendship between the Vikings and the Assiniboine and Cree Nations.

Thorhilde at once understood that if she rejected the offer, she would have made enemies of both the two tribes. She asked inside herself for guidance from the Lord in order to get help to tackle the situation. She smiled and said to the Chiefs "Of course we can help you, how many horses do you want?"

The chiefs looked happy and turned to their advisers and said "How many horses do you have?"

"Right now we have some eighty horses, but some of the mares will be pregnant during the winter and the best gift that we can give you is eight pregnant mares and two young stallions. They can reproduce the flock for you."

"Thank you very much, how many swords and bows with arrows can you give us?" the chiefs continued.

"We can give you six swords and six bows with arrows, the rest we need ourselves."

They didn't like that answer and were counseling among the others.

"We had hoped for more weapons." They said angrily.

Thorhilde felt that she had stretched herself far enough and said "We are utterly dependent upon our weapons to survive, as a compensation we can provide you with food for the winter."

It softened the heated arguments among the native chiefs and eventually the Assiniboine and Cree Chiefs nodded in agreement and said "We have another proposal to you, all three of us will cut our hands and shake hands and share our blood as a token of us becoming true friends and one family. We also want two of our daughters to become married to two of your young warriors, one Assiniboine Princess and one Cree Princess. They are young, innocent and beautiful and will be coming along with you on your journey south. This shall also be as a token of our friendship and also that you will never forget us. Also I have one more plea for you "We have among us a very young girl that have been thrown out by the Blackfeet because of abnormalities to her body and to her mind. They call her Sadbird. Can you take her with you and try to mend her abnormalities? Perhaps you can ask your White God for help?"

"Of course, I will gladly adopt her as my own daughter!" Can you please assign me someone to teach us the Siouan language as well as provide us with a scout for our journey southwards?" Thorhilde asked the Chiefs. "Horses and weapons you will receive some time next summer."

"Good! We will see to that someone will come and teach you our language and we will bring you Ugly before you leave." This was the last word from the Chiefs.

After the natives had left Thorhilde summoned the settlers for a grand counsel. She recited everything to the households and asked for their opinion on what she had agreed upon. One of the men asked her "Can we afford to lose that many horses? You have already promised them four horses and weapons in Greenland!"

"We have to use our mares only for breeding purposes and use the oxen for any heavy work. Today we have some sixty mares and they should be able to reproduce the eight in addition to the four that we promised in Greenland."

"What will you do if they come for more horses later." The same man asked in a mild tone.

"Maybe offer them a couple of older stallions. I will not let either of the chiefs intimidate or fool me."

"However what I feel more concern about is that we must not give away any more swords, and rather also not bows and arrows. We will need them ourselves."

"Who are you to propose us to marry any of us to the chief's daughters? We are borne free! one of the younger men asked.

"Are you becoming frightened Haakon, Thorhilde asked the young man directly, or are you hoping that I might ask you? They are probably young beauties!"

"The elderly native women look battered and beaten." He said with a smile on his face.

"That is because of hard work and insufficient nourishment. But I have a feeling that you will see to that your Native wife will be properly treated Haakon."

"You said my Native wife!"

"Yes I did Haakon! I will here and now ask that you volunteer to become the first one in this settlement to take a Native Bride. It is of great importance that we form a good relationship with the natives. What do you say?"

"Since you are our Queen, I can probably not reject." Haakon answered with a smile on his face. When can I see her and when will we get married."

"Come summer after we are done with our planting and sowing I will arrange with the Assiniboine Chief for the weddings and for the exchange of gifts. The natives call it Potluck."

"Will you also give some of our daughters to the Natives." one of the mothers asks.

"I will not do that. They will not be treated well by their husbands; probably they will be treated like slaves."

The settlers went home to their humble homes, pondering in their harts all the events that had taken place, but now with peace in their minds.

One morning when the snow is deep in the fields, Thorhilde is awakened by alarming news. "Please come immediately. Gyda is very sick and is probably dying," a younger woman, almost in tears, begged her.

Thorhilde rushes to Gyda's little hut and almost immediately sees that she has not long to live. She is breathing very heavily and has a livid facial color.

She tries to smile to Thorhilde and to look courageous. "How are you today my little Sunshine?"

Thorhilde kneels down by the bed and folds her hands in utter agony and pleads with the Lord to let her grandmother become well again. "Please Dear Lord! Help her! The tears flow down her cheeks and she put her wet chins close to her grandmother's face. She stays in this position for hours and has to become very gently removed by a couple of attending women.

"Your grandmother has gone to her forefathers Thorhilde." One of them tells her gently." You must move so that we can dress her."

Thorhilde takes control of herself and knows that she has to act like a Queen. She thinks of all the good time that they have had together and of all the fantastic advice that she has received from her grandmother. Most of all she remembers the love that Gyda unselfishly showered her with over so many years. I have been so lucky to have had her beside me for so long. She thanks the Lord again and again for the time that she and Gyda have had together.

After Gyda had been dressed and everyone in the settlement had an opportunity to come and see her for the last time, Thorhilde asks the women attending, to leave her alone with her grandmother for the night. The funeral was already arraigned for the next day. Being alone with the dead body did not frighten her at all. She felt only peaceful. She recited the commandments of the Lord as she had done so many times before when her Grandmother listened to every word. Then she recites with a solemn, respectful and shivering voice from the book of Job, "The Lord hat given and the Lord hat taken away. Blessed is the name of the Lord." She eventually falls to sleep beside the ready made coffin with her grandmother inside.

This is how she is found by her uncle and his wife the next morning. They gently awakened her and tell her that she has to cherish the good times that they had together. They tell her that Gyda had been struggling with breast pain for some time but they had promised her not to tell Thorhilde, because of all the important tasks that she as a Queen had to take care of. Gyda lived a good life and came to a good age. She told us that she so much appreciated you Thorhilde, for everything that you meant to her. Your courage, kindness, control of temper and diligence in promoting the commandments of the Lord, meant so much to her Thorhilde."

The funeral the next day takes place a crisp December day. Snow has fallen and the scenery outside is gorgeous. Snow has made the earlier grey and dull landscape look like a winter palace, and the frost has decorated the trees and brushes in a way almost unthinkable, but only to be seen. Thorhilde manages to take in the beauty of the land and to feel happy inside. Now her grandmother is in a place even more beautiful than here and free of pain and worries.

Guttorm now becoming old is conducting the ceremony. He tells everyone about the good attributes of Gyda, her concern for the well being of all the settlers, her wisdom, knowledge, diligence and courage. He says "Most of all I admire here for her compassion towards anyone who does not have a mother and a father or a large extended family around them. She is gone to her husband that she lost so early in her marriage and to her long awaiting and loving parents. May we all follow her example of love, compassion and diligence in our lives. May the Lord be with her soul?"

Thorhilde watches in solemn silence as the coffin is being sunk into the frozen prairie ground. She has no more tears to shed. She goes home to herself and braces herself for her future loneliness.

The winter is gone and the short spring has arrived in the Winnipeg Settlement. It is already mid April 1329 and most of the snow is gone. Some of the spring flowers have appeared and nature is looking beautiful. There is the green grass with spring flowers, the evergreen spruces and pines. Some of the trees are still have dots of snow displaying their beauty to the world. Birds are singing in the trees again and fresh water is breaking the barriers of ice that restrained it during the winter. A whole new creation is taking place before the eyes of all of the settlers. A merciful and compassionate Lord has given us this beautiful land to dress, till and harvest. May we become worthy of being here.

Come May the settlers had already started to sow and plant. They knew that they would leave the settlement early next May for Minnesota and that they needed to have everything in good working order before they were to leave.

Thorhilde had been asked by Olaf, the son of Bjarni, if he could become the bridegroom to the daughter of the Cree Chief. He told her that his own family had disowned him and that he saw no future with them. I will cast my lot with a Cree native as well as with you in the future. I shall always be faithful to you my Queen.

"Unfortunately I have already asked Sigvat, and he has accepted it. You have to stick with me as my personal guard." She again feels very sorry for him! "It can't be helped" he answers "As your personal guard, I will protect you with my life if necessary." He then tells Thorhilde that his father Bjarni had come to him in disguise the last night before he was executed and asked him to murder both her and Gyda in their sleep and to promote him Olaf as their new Leader and King.

"Why didn't you warn me?"

Thorhilde asked in surprise.

"I thought of it for a while but wanted to see him play his cards out as well as to see who was with him. If he would have attacked you, I would have stopped him. Also I wanted everyone at the Thing to truly see what kind of man that he had become, including my own family. By the way I informed your grandmother of it and she made the necessary precautions to make you safe."

"Olaf, I know that you did what you thought was the best for me and that you are a true friend of me. We are all safe now, but I am truly sorry that the outcome of my conflict with your father should come to this."

"He brought this upon himself all alone. No one is to blame for his open rebellion against you, but himself." Olaf seems to accept the verdict that the Thing placed upon his own father.

The spring came and disappeared fast and now summer is here already. The day for the wedding is coming close and a lot of preparations have been made to make it a real happy and an event to be remembered. Thorhilde are having some of the younger men and girls training in the Old Norwegian folk dances, a tradition that the settlers of Greenland cherished and kept alive. She also knew that both the Assiniboine and Cree natives were to bring dancers, all dressed in their national customs, to dance and amuse them all. The Vikings were to stay close to their weapons if anything unpleasant was to happen, but she did not anticipate it.

Good food was to be made both the Native way as well as the Norwegian way. She was really looking forward to the grand fiesta. The women had made beautiful dresses for both themselves and for gifts for the brides. All horses were to be decorated and the two couples were planned to leave the ceremony on horseback to their newly erected homes in the Viking Settlement, but this was only to be done after the show of dancers had performed to their finish and a lot of good food had been served and consumed. Thorhilde had strictly forbidden any serving of intoxicating beverage to anyone, for she knew well the effect it had upon the natives. In fairness, they also had to forbid it to the Viking settlers as well.

It was now already mid June and she admired the land of Hope and Glory that she had dreamed about for many years. The vast prairie and the magnificent forests as well as the beautiful rivers, made her singing as she walked along the river. Her personal guard was always s close to her. At least two of them were always so close that they could come to her immediate assistance if a situation should occur that she could not handle alone. She knew well that she had enemies among her own and also knew that the natives could suddenly turn on her for an unpredictable reason. Also she remembered that "Success brings faked friends and true enemies." She started to think of who were her faked friends, but couldn't think of any in particular. However she knew some of her enemies. In particular the three families that were fined at the Thing were not her friends, but much more likely her enemies.

She didn't think that they would try to harm her bodily, but were more apt to sabotage her decisions in any sly way they could imagine. I will be on my guard always she thought to herself. Gyda was wise to teach me to contemplate any upcoming danger. When we are to leave for Minnesota next spring, we must be prepared for raids against us. The Dakota Sioux will not be as friendly as the Assiniboine and the Cree are. I pray to the Lord we will survive their open aggression against any trespassing of their hunting grounds. In a way, she understood their feelings. It was their land and how would the Vikings have reacted if it was their land and someone else suddenly wanted admission to it. She knew well these thoughts wouldn't do well with the Viking settlers. Understandably she had to keep them to herself.

Midsummer Day had arrived and the atmosphere was explosive. The settlers were all nicely dressed and in their best behavior as they were streaming to the open and beautiful decorated field where the wedding ceremony was to be held. At the very same place later in the day, the dance shows would be displayed and there would be a final grand eating fiesta for all. As a grand finale, the two couples were to depart on horsebacks.

The day arrived and Thorhilde arrived on horseback dressed the same way as she was at her crowning in the Northwestern Settlement of Greenland. She was a sight be admired by many of the people present both settlers and Assiniboine and Cree alike. Following her was her own personal guard as well as fifty warriors, all of them mounted and armed. Their armor, shields, swords and spears had all been shined and sparkled in the sun. She dismounted and presented to the native chiefs the gifts of horses and weapons that she had promised earlier, and then greeted Guttorm and the two couples warmly.

They had all agreed on having three ceremonies, one Christian, one Assiniboine and one Cree. Excitement could be felt everywhere as the different people awaited the day's activities.The church ceremony was very touching for everyone present. Due to lack of space only close families were invited inside, but a huge crowed was waiting outside to cheer the newly wed. It was quite a sight to watch the beautiful dressed brides and all the very colorful dressed natives with all their beautiful hair ornaments of different kinds, all of them watching reverently.

Time finally arrived for the native ceremonies, first an Assiniboine ceremony for Haakon and his Assiniboine bride and then a Cree ceremony for Sigvat and his Cree bride. It was all very respectfully conducted and many of the spectators had tears in their eyes when all the wedding ceremonies were done with.

After the weddings ceremonies the young dancers from the settlement performed Old Norwegian folk dances for them, and the Assiniboine and Cree natives watched in wonder. The native dancers had a fantastic display, and the settlers were exited and amused by them and their music.

Rounding the day off was a gorgeous fiesta with the best of food, before the two married couples left for their new homes on horseback, and the day ended with the natives and the settlers going back to their homes.

Chapter VIII

On the Top of the World and Singing Grass – 1330

The winter had passed away and a lot of learning activities had kept them well occupied. Thorhilde had emphasized the learning of the native languages as the most important subject, and they were all doing fairly well. Also a lot of time had past by with telling stories about ancient people and also about superstitious and mystic signs and wanders. She knew very well that the settlers were both deeply religious and at the same time also very superstitious, and that they many times intermixed the two of them.

Spring had finally arrived, the snow had melted and the settlers were all busy in preparing for the departure up the south fork of the Winnipeg River with all their ships, animals and belongings. Their native Assiniboine scout informs them that the river will lead them to the Top of the World.

"What do you mean by that?" Thorhilde asked him in broken Siouan language.

"When we have followed the river to its origin, we will enter a plateau where three large water systems originate. We will then leave the Winnipeg water system that includes the South Winnipeg River, Winnipeg Lake, and the Saskatchewan River with all its tributaries, the North Winnipeg River, the Large Winnipeg Bay, The Winnipeg Strait between Helluland(Baffin Island) and Markland(Labrador) and finally the Large Ocean Strait between this continent and Greenland. To the south of the Top of the World we will enter into an enormous water system of some large rivers. We will first enter into the southbound mother of the rivers the mighty Mississippi. Close to the Mississippi River but somewhat further west flows another great river the Minnesota River that The Dakota Sioux have named and also signifies the region that surround the Minnesota River. The Mississippi gets its name from the natives of this continent and the meaning is that she is the very origin to the fertility of this vast region of this continent. The Mississippi is fed by some very important children on its way towards the ocean far to the south. It is fed by the Wisconsin River and the Illinois River and after having passed in rage over the Mississippi Rapids it is nourished by its very oldest son, the large, wild and unpredictable Missouri River. Later on, it is fed by its oldest daughter the large and beautiful Ohio River that is again being fed by a granddaughter of the Mississippi River, the Tennessee River. Many other smaller sons and daughters to The Mississippi River support their mother with water during its journey down to the ocean. Her children also have sons and daughters feeding them again, and they again have children and grandchildren feeding them too. Anciently they all promised by oath that their mother river should never dry up. To the east of the Top of the World there is a large water system of five very large Lakes. The shortest route to reach them is straight east from the Top of the World to the largest and coldest of the lakes that we natives calls the Great Lake, but the easiest way, especially with the ships that you are having with you, is the far more longer route down the Mississippi River to the Illinois River. Then upstream the Illinois River unto it almost hooks up with the south loop of the Chicago River."

He continuous, "some time later, an important village will be built there, because it connects two large water systems. The Chicago River empties into the large Lake Michigan. By travelling north as far as you can and then turn east you will come to Lake Huron that will take you south to a river channel into Lake Erie. At its eastern end there is a tremendous waterfall that the natives call Niagara. To bypass that you will have to drag your ships overland down to Lake Ontario. The natives of this region are Iroquois speaking and very warlike and I have heard that your people already know them from earlier journeys in that region. To the south of Lake Erie you will meet the Erie's that are fearful warriors and infamous for being the only tribe on this continent to use poisonous arrows. Stay away from them if you can. On the north side of Lake Ontario, the Huron Nation has their hunting grounds and to the south side of the lake, five Iroquois tribes have their hunting grounds. Four of the tribes the Seneca, the Cayuga, the Oneida and the Onondaga have their main villages close to the Finger Lakes. The fifth of them the Mohawks live some further east on the Mohawk River. All these tribes are in a defense coalition and are dreadful enemies. Please stay away from them," he warns. "Lake Ontario empties into a large river that continuous north east into a large bay and further out into the open ocean. I know that your people have traveled many times over the big lakes that way. My ancestors have told me many stories from their encounters while trading with us."

When they are all ready to depart southward up river, a group of Assiniboine and Cree Natives approach them for a farewell ceremony. They are bringing with them small gifts and Talismans that are to protect them against evil spirits and mortal enemies on their journey trough life. Talismans being small amulets that is supposed to bring good luck. Thorhilde thanks them warmly for their care and are almost touched by their sincerity and care for their well beings.

Suddenly she comes to see that they have a little girl with them. She cannot be more than six years old and has a very unhappy look on her face. Then Thorhilde remembers her promise to the Native Chiefs. This surely must be Sadbird, the little girl that she promised to take with her. Thorhilde knelt down and beckoned to the little girl to approach her. As she did, the girl understood she was to be her mother.

The girl was little and uncomely to look at. Sadbird had a sour look in her very dark brown face and looked like she had missed too many meals. She looked unhappy, rejected, scared and suspicious and probably did not believe that anyone, anywhere would love and comfort her. Her new mother to be immediately felt love and compassion for her and managed to catch her very dark brown eyes and to keep eye contact with her. Generally the little girl would turn away from eye contact for fear of rejection. Nobody had ever loved her, and she did not remember her own Blackfoot mother or family.

Thorhilde took the little girl with her to her quarter to sleep the last night before they were to depart early next morning the first day of May 1330. She undressed the little girl and saw that she had bruises both on her back as well as on her butt and legs. One of legs was slightly deformed causing s slight limp.

Thorhilde almost cried when she saw the state that she was in." How could anybody do such a thing to a little defenseless child?" She thought to herself. "Stay with me little darling and I will house you and love you and care for you."

It is almost as if the little girl understands her Old Norse language because her face lightens up like a lamp in darkness and a little smile wrinkles her dark brown face. Thorhildes heart almost sparkles together with the little smiling face of the girl. The little girl points towards herself and acclaim in her Siouan language "My name is Sadbird, and I am ugly, what is your name?"

"I am Thorhilde, but you are not ugly, you are beautiful!" Thorhilde answers in broken Siouan.

"No I am not beautiful. Everybody tells me that I am ugly!"

"Then they are not telling you the truth darling. I can both see and feel your beauty!" Thorhilde says emotionally.

"How can you see that I am not ugly? Everybody else tells me that I am ugly and unlovable?" the little girl asks with surprise in her voice.

"Those people that have told you such a thing cannot have studied you closely enough!" Thorhilde is very convincing in her voice.

"I find it hard to believe you!" the little girl looks suspicious.

"Can you tell me who has been beating you?" Thorhilde points to her bruises.

The little girl's facial expression immediately turns from normal happy to seriously sad and she goes into a complete silence.

Thorhilde understand that she needs to give her more time and to gain her trust and confidence before she could question her on her unpleasant past life. "I think that the two of us shall go to bed, but first of all you need a good cleaning." She helped Sadbird to wash and dry both body as well as hair and found some cloths that were far to large for her but would have to do until she could find something that were more suitable for her.

"The two of us will sleep together for the time coming." Thorhilde said warmly to the little Blackfoot girl.

"I have never been allowed to sleep with anyone before. All I had was a blanket on the floor to sleep on. Why are you so nice to me?" Sadbird is surprised.

"Because I like you and love you little darling, and you shall be the new daughter that the Lord has now proved me to replace the daughter that I lost when she was small. She would have been about your age now if she had been allowed to live. Thorhilde answers her sad but smilingly.

Sadbird seems to be taken by surprise and then asks "What was her name?"

"Her name was Thorgunn after my mother who died in childbirth with me."

"How sad!", Sadbird exclaims.

"By the way" Thorhilde says "I do not like the name Sadbird, I want to rename you Singing Grass"

"Why that name." The little girl is surprised.

"You remind me of the beauty of the prairie grass and the sweet sound that a sharp ear can hear when the wind blows through it.'" Thorhilde says.

"I really like that name, but do you think that the rest of the children will also feel it that way" She asks suspicious again.

"I am sure that they will!" Thorhilde says with confidence in her voice.

The next morning the little flotilla of some twenty ships started on its southward journey. "The Dragon of Greenland "was in the lead with the twenty smaller family ships and the two support ships following. The ships were rowed against the stream fully crewed and the cattle was herded along the river banks. To protect the settlers, ships, equipment and cattle Thorhilde ordered the horses to be mounted with armed warriors and to flank the cattle against any sudden attack from Dakota Sioux Natives.

Thorhilde herself was on horseback and fully armed.

They proceeded from early morning to late night with only short stops for food and drinks. When the night came they found a good defensive place to camp for the night. They tied the ships together in full battle formation and made a defensive circle around the camp. Very cautiously they placed all their animals between the ships and the rest of the camp.

The settlers had named their Assiniboine scout after their Nordic God Odin, since they were not capable of pronouncing his real name. He told them that the Dakotas would operate in small bands of war parties and could attack them at any given moment if they were not alert. One strategy that they would employ was to scare the animals so much that they would stampede and run away. He strongly advised the settlers to tie all animals so tight that they would not be able to escape.

Thorhilde was very pleased with him and thanked the Lord for being so lucky as to have such a good scout and adviser with them.

Further on Odin advised them that the native Dakota could apply several tricks to unsettle and shake them up. They could dress in wolf hides and let the cattle smell the danger and stampede, or make such a racket as to scare them away. Odin also advise them that they should bring their children and their animals onboard the ships and have the animals lie down and tie them up for the night if they felt that they were in mortal danger. Then let the most experienced archers man the ships and let the rest of the settlers meet the Native warriors on the river banks.

Thorhilde asked Odin if he thought that they were going to be attacked and he answered "For sure they will attack us if they feel certain of a victory. They are constantly watching us for that purpose. I can hear their war cries by night and their signals by night already. After a week along the south loop of the Winnipeg River, we will turn east leaving the Winnipeg River and crossing the Top of the World to the beginning of the mother of all rivers, the Mighty Mississippi River."

And he continuous "Up there we will probably be more safe against attack from The Native Dakotas. It is not the best of their hunting grounds and is so barren that it doesn't give them much vegetation to creep in on us. Why don't we find a good campsite by the very beginning of the Mississippi River and rest there for a few days before we proceed further south following the Mississippi"

The crossing was laborious for the settlers. All the ships had to be pulled across prairieland. However they were experienced people and had done this many times before. After days of hard labor they are happy to find a good campsite alongside a small lake.

"Here we will rest for some days," Thorhilde orders.

As the days goes by Thorhilde now have ample time to become acquainted with the little Blackfoot orphan girl Singing Grass.

"How have your time with us been so far Darling she asks Singing Grass!"

"The other children mock me mother. They tell me that I am dark, dirty and ugly and they cannot understand why you have brought me along with you."

Thorhilde gets stunned with anger on her behalf, but knows inside herself that children can behave very cruelly towards each others, especially girls towards other girls. She thinks to herself "Maybe children picks on other children to avoid becoming picked on themselves. Strangely it may be a sort of self protection."

She asks gently "Who is it that is saying this to you. Is it the boys or the girls or both of them?"

"It is really all of the children." The little Blackfoot girl answers 'but the girls are the most evil ones." Then she continues "Don't cry mother, I love you and you are nice to me. I am use to being mocked. It doesn't hurt me anymore."

Thorhilde cannot restrain her feelings anymore and takes the little girl on her lap and hold her tight into her and begins to weep. After some time they both fall asleep close together.

When the little girl are sound asleep by night she summons the heads of the households and in very frank words tells them what she thinks of the behavior of their children and asks for them to have it stopped. Almost all of them agrees with her and say that they will restrain their children but a few of them tells her that they will not interfere. Especially the three families that were fined for their support of Bjarni are reluctant to cooperate and Thorhilde knows now that they will always be her enemies. Bjarnis widow is especially reluctant to consider any reprimands for her children for any wrong doing towards the little Blackfoot girl. Thorhilde understand that this is one of her ways of making a revenge of Bjarni, and that nothing is to low for having revenge.

"Don't you have any compassion for that poor little girl?" she asks Bjarnis widow with surprise in her voice.

"Nothing at all, if you want to take care of that little half human creature, so let it be so, but do not pester us with your bad conscious for your hardship towards Bjarni."

"You need to have your mouth washed Ragnhilde!" Thorhilde answered cold as ice. "If you do not know how to do it, I can arrange for having that done to you!"

Ragnhilde screams out and looks like she is ready to attack Thorhilde, and is stopped by to of the men.

Before Ragnhilde is escorted out she shouts out all the filthy words that she knows and also curses Thorhilde to death.

When they are all quiet down again, Thorhilde asks for the support of the head of the households to stop all mobbing of Singing Grass for the future. She says "We are Christians and have taken an oath to live our lives the Christian way. This oath is the highest of all oaths and bypasses any oath to sovereigns, church leaders or landlords, even to mothers and fathers. Clearly we as intelligent and enlightened Christians cannot sit idly and watch a little native orphan girl be mistreated and called bad names by our children" Everyone present but the three families agrees to support her.

Thorhilde has not given in to trying to reason with the remaining two families. She says "If you are angry with me, why take it out on this innocent child?"

"Shall I be completely honest with you my Queen." one of the men says.

"Please be so honest!" Thorhilde answers.

"I don't like you or anything that you stand for!" the man says angrily.

"You are entitled to an opinion Herjulf, but please try to cooperate with me. I am your elected Queen and am trying my best to secure the well being for all of us."

"I believe that you are so my Queen the man answered but do not try to pressure us to like the little Blackfoot girl, because we don't." The man answered flatly."

"I cannot force you to like anyone Herjulf, but please try to cooperate with me. Is there anything that I can do for you to ease the strain that have developed between us?"

"Yes there is one thing more that you can do, don't let any more of our young men and woman marry into native families. We want to keep our Nordic blood clean!"

"Herjulf you are trying to make the marriages of Haakon and Sigvat to Assiniboine and Cree Princesses look dirty. Are you aware of it that we have Israeli as well as Scythian and Irish blood in us?"

"They were at least white people!' the man continued stubbornly.

"Are you aware of that hunters and traders from our Northwestern Settlement in Greenland have fathered hundreds of Aleut and Inuit Eskimo children, and those traders and settlers from the Southeastern Settlement of Greenland have intermixed with the Cherokees, Ho Chunk and several other eastern tribes for centuries? Are you aware of that the Mandan's are half Nordic?"

"That doesn't mean that we have to follow suit in their wrong doings. We are not coming here all the way from Greenland to start fathering half breeds!" The man wouldn't give in easily.

"Are you aware of that you are blackening all of their offspring's?"

"I am just telling you the truth, take it or leave it! Herjulf got himself up and left.

Thorhilde was stunned but knew well that it was better to have it out in the open as early as possible, and she also knew that it was discussed among the settlers and that many of them supported Herjulf, though not openly. Also she understood that the subject was too touchy to ask them to have a vote on it, only time and wisdom could ever solve it.

They all left for their homes and Thorhilde was shaken to her backbones. As she came to her quarters she saw the little Blackfoot girl sound asleep with a pleasant smile on her face and suddenly she felt that all evil had disappeared from her and her little makeshift home. She didn't undress but kept her weapons ready by her side. Before she went to sleep next to Singing Grass she asked two of her personal guards to be on high alert and also asked for a doubling of the guards of warriors.

Having slept a few hours she awakened with an uneasy feeling and arose. She saw her two guards standing talking and asked them to watch over the little girl, while she went to wake Odin.

He was already up and listening cautiously. Obviously something was far wrong.

Thorhilde immediately wakened the warriors and asked them to arm and stay alert. "Wake up the families silently and guard the animals" she ordered.

Suddenly they were awakened by high pitched screams and a shower of arrows coming. Now all the settlers were on full alert and ready. So far none of them had been seriously injured and none of the animals had started to move. Then they saw that the next move of the Dakotas was to burn them out. They were already starting a fire, but did not realize that the settlers had anticipated such a move. A counter fire was started immediately and the two fires met and consumed each others quickly.

The fires lightened the horizon so much that the settlers could clearly see some hundreds warriors in the background pulling slowly away in disappointment.

When the daylight came the next morning they were able to assess the damage. None of the settlers had been hit by the arrows but one horse and one cow had to be put down due to bad wounds. A horse had got an arrow straight in his eye and a cow had an arrow through her throat. They were both in great pain and were quickly relieved by death. Before they left they slaughtered the animals for food and preserved it for the journey.

Thorhilde seeks out Olaf and asks him if he is alright. "I have been worried for you Olaf she says and hugs him warmly. You have had your father put to death and your mother has disowned you in public, and I can't stand to see more evil happen to you. You are such a remarkable sturdy and nice young man. Only at the age of eighteen, you are more matured than most men around here. I wish that my son Yngve had lived and become like you."

"Thank you, my Queen!", Olaf answers.

The settlers were called together and they all understood that they had to be united and alert. Early morning they continued south in the same formation ay as they had had earlier. Now they are proceeding downriver and the journey is far easier but they are always on their guard against attack. Eventually they arrive at the junction where the Mississippi River meets the Minnesota River and they settled for a few days on the high bluffs on the northern side.

Thorhilde feels like they all need a rest and they meet and agree to a couple of days off to gather strength and to reorganize themselves. There is no need for Thorhilde to reemphasize the need for alertness. They are all aware of it.

She now takes a lot of time together with Singing Grass. After the meeting that she had with the settlers about children behavior, life has been much better for the little Blackfoot girl. Bad words are seldom being spoken and most of the time the children are actually nice to her.

Thorhilde is brushing her long coal black hair and is helping her setting it up beautifully. The atmosphere in the quarter is tranquil and pleasant.

"Singing Grass, tell me about your life with the Blackfoot tribe as you remember it, will you?"

"Why do you want to know that mother?"

"In order to understand you little girl, I need to understand your past as well."

"So what do you want to know mother?"

"Tell me about your Blackfoot mother!"

"I don't remember her all that much, but I do remember that she had a lot of problems."

Thorhilde asks mildly "What kind of problems did your mother have darling?"

"She was always being told by other members of the tribe that she ought to get rid of me!" Singing Grass replied with sorrow in her voice.

"What was the reason for your mother to be told of such an awful thing?" Thorhilde ask with horror in her voice.

"They all said that I was deformed and ugly looking and that no man would ever want me for his wife, and that it had been far better for everyone that I had never been born."

"What happened then darling girl?"

"They were discussing if they should set me out for wild animals to devour me or if they could sell me to one of the neighboring tribes. One day some Assiniboine tribe's people came along and felt sorry for me. They took me with them to the Chief and he sincerely tried to help me, but the children were not nice to me."

"That was very nice of the Assiniboine and not so nice of your own tribe. Are you very mad with your own mother?"

"Not really!" Singing Grass answer with sadness in her voice "She tried the best she could to care for me but the rest of the tribe pressured her beyond her breaking point. In the next life I will have two mothers, you and her, is not that something to look forward to?"

"You are a beautiful child little darling, both outside and inside!" Thorhilde said with passion in her voice.

"What was your mother's name?"

"Her name is almost the same as the name that you gave me. The name is Whispering Grass. Do you think that I will ever see her in this life mother?"

"Those names are both beautiful. Have you got a Blackfoot name for me"?

"Yes I have mother, may I call you Bleeding Heart?"

"Why will you call me that darling?"

"Because your hart bleeds for both me and for my mother!", the little Blackfoot girl says it with a stern voice and with a big smile on her face. She stretches out her little arms towards Thorhilde and they both embrace each others. "Bleeding Heart, I know for sure now that you love both me and my poor mother, and may the Creator of all things bless you forever. You are the only person that really has loved me and appreciated my company."

"That was really beautiful darling!" Thorhilde smiles and thanks her warmly. "I have never in my life before heard anything so beautiful."

The little Blackfoot girl smiles and says "I need to sleep now Bleeding Heart. Good night. I love you!"

"I love you too Singing Grass. Good night and sleep well!"

The settlers stay a couple of days on the bluff where they have a perfect view of the two rivers and the surrounding area. They are now in late May and if they are to plant for the season in their final settlement they are better to start moving down river fast. They all agree on a settlement on the river Ohio, where they have had good reports from earlier settlers.

The next morning the settlers are on the move down the Mississippi River. To speed up the journey they put all the children and the elderly as well as the slow moving animals onboard the ships and have all the horses and the fast moving animals follow on the river banks. The ships are crewed with sailors and oarsmen and also with the best archers, ready to support the men and animals on the river banks.

Eighty warriors are mounted, armed and ready to guard the far flank of the livestock and the whole little army are moving at a good speed.

The tenth of June 1330 they have been journeying for almost three weeks and are now at the Mississippi Rapids where they have to discharge of all cargo in order to have the ships come safely through. It does not take all that long, but all equipment has to be freighted passed the rapids on horseback or carried manually. The whole event takes a full day and the settlers take a day to rest afterwards in order to gain strength for the further voyage.

Thorhilde counsel with the settlers and asks them on what day they consider the last day that they can successfully plant in Ohio. One man that has been there earlier tells them that the climate along the Ohio River is very mild and that the very fertile soil will allow them a harvest even if they should plant in early July.

She spends the afternoon with Singing Grass and tries to heal her wounds on our feet by applying an ointment that Odin has recommended. He has this knowledge from the tribal medicine man and knows from experience that it may work if it is applied regularly over a long time. When Thorhilde asked him if the Blackfoot also had this knowledge, he answered that they probably had this knowledge, but that the family of her mother were either too lazy or too ignorant to even try it.

"Can you please show me where I will find these plants, and also how to make this ointment when we arrive in our next settlement?"

"Of course I will Thorhilde" he answered smilingly. "You will make both her body and her spirit whole again with your true love and kindness."

"Thank you Odin!" she thanked him wholeheartedly for his kind and encouraging words.

After she has anointed the little girl, Thorhilde takes a long time in brushing the hair of Singing Grass. She wants so much to make the little girl look beautiful and to regain her self esteem.

Thorhilde brings out her beautiful mirror and say to Singing Grass "Who is that beautiful girl that you are seeing in the mirror. Is that anyone that you know?"

The little Blackfoot girl giggles and says "But Bleeding Heart, you know that the girl is me."

"I do, but can you also see that you are beautiful too?"

Singing Grass hesitates for a moment and blurts out "If there is beauty in me, you are the one that has made it come out! Can I stay with you forever?"

"Of course you can darling!"

"Can my mother be with us too?" Singing Grass says in a pleading voice.

"I promise you darling that your mother can stay with us as well" Thorhilde answers the little girl.

"Let us have something to eat and then go to bed early. We have a long journey ahead of us."

Chapter IX

The Shawnee and the final settlement by the Ohio River – 1330 –

After several days of laborious journeying the traveling party arrives at a place where there already is a small settlement of x-Greenlanders.

They are heartily welcomed and everyone in the settlement is eager to meet their new Queen and to hear news of the expedition. After they are all settled and rested Guttorm summons everyone to hear him speak.

He says "We are now coming together as friends and fellow Christians to organize our permanent settlement in this land that our Icelandic friends and family calls Vinland, meaning the land with the good pastures. By the mercy of an everlasting and omnipotent God we have arrived here without suffering much harm. We were forced by nature, injustice and political events in Europe to leave our beautiful Northwestern Settlement in Greenland in order for us to survive both mortally and as free men. On my advice the men and women of the Northwestern Settlement of Greenland elected the childless widow Thorhilde Arnfinsdaughter as our Queen and to lead us during the preparation, migration and establishment in this choice land. She is of noble and in legal marriage descent from the King of Norway, the High King of Ireland and the clan chiefs of both Clan MacLeod and Clan MacDonald of the Western Isles of Scotland. Her upbringing has given her the knowledge of foreign lands, the history of our ancient forefathers as well as a good working knowledge of the Nordic language. She also has the knowledge of Latin sufficient to read and understand the Holy Scriptures.Throughout her lifetime she has lived a sober and God fearing life.

She has been very diligent in keeping all the commandments of the Lord and has always had compassion for the weak and the needy. When we were considering whom we should ask to take upon him or her enormous responsibility, the choice of her became clearer for each day that we were considering it. Even how much we dislike the royalties and its offspring the aristocracy, we did and still do see the necessity of her reign over us during her lifetime so that we may become properly organized and protected during this important and dangerous time for us and for our descendants. Her "kingdom" will only last for her lifetime and she has agreed to never remarry or to have any offspring that might challenge for a succession of the "kingdom".

During our stay in the Winnipeg Settlement, Bjarni Thorvaldson rebelled openly against her and was sentenced to the sword by the Thing. I know that the three families that were in support of Bjarni and were fined for that are still harboring resentment against Thorhilde. They are probably likely to spread lies of her and will also probably fabricate intrigues as well as sabotage her decisions. Please do not become a part of these destructive behaviors.We learned later on from Bjarni,s son Olaf that his father came to him by night and asked him to kill both Thorhilde and her grandmother Gyda silently by night and that Bjarni would then present him Olaf Bjarnison as their new king. Olaf is present here and will verify this for you after I have spoken to you. If you wonder why no one has revealed this to you earlier I can assure you that there was no intention of secrecy of it, but to wait until we were all safe and gathered together. Though you probably all do feel that the decision by the Thing to put him to the sword was a harsh decision, it did become necessary. Had it not been for the honesty and integrity of Olaf, Bjarni might have succeeded in his devious plan.

I will also take the time to educate you in something that has become a talking point among you. Are we to allow our young men and daughters to be given away in marriage to our native friends? There is considerable concern among you of their safety and well being, and I fully understand that. It is whatsoever way we might see it far better to father children within wedlock, than outside of wedlock. Please look very hard upon the character of any native girl or boy that might come into question as a son or daughter in law, and do not have any prejudices towards skin colors, family background, religion or origin. Only one thing I will do advise you to, have them becoming properly married and thought and skilled in our ways. If they choose to leave our settlement and go their own ways, please do not disown them but love them and welcome them back if they want to return to you. Probably you feel that this might never happen to you, remember that you are now in a new world and are surrounded by tens of thousands of natives that you must learn how to live among in order to survive.

Please go home and think deeply about this and if you are not sure go, in solemn prayer to the Lord himself and ask him directly. I vouch for Thorhildes integrity and for everything that she stands for, and I will be very pleased if we all recite the ceremony of the crowning in the Northwestern Settlement of Greenland here in Vinland. Will everyone that is in acceptance of reciting the ceremony step forward?"

Almost immediately everyone but the three families steps forward and shout "We want Thorhilde as our Queen and want the ceremony to be performed."

Olaf Bjarnison then addresses them and says. "I am very sad to bring this news to you about my own father, but he truly came to me that night in question and asked me to silently kill both Thorhilde and Gyda. He promised me in return the kingdom. I did tell Gyda about it and she put extra guards out for Thorhildes protection during the next day of Thing. He then acted so rebellious, violent and disrespectful that a proposal was put forward to the Thing by one of the other families to put him to the sword because he was so offensive and dangerous that he could put us all in jeopardy. At that time the Thing did not know of him coming to me in disguise the former night asking me to assassinate Thorhilde and Gyda. I was ready to address the Thing and tell everyone the whole story, but Gyda advised me to wait and see how my father played his cards out. Afterwards I can see that it was wisdom in her advice to me, but I had a very difficult time in seeing my own father becoming beheaded. Now my own family has disowned me, but I am happy with my life.

One of the Ohio settlers asks Olaf "Do you think that your mother knew what your father was up to?"

"I do not think that she knew of his plot to have Thorhilde and Gyda killed but I do think that she knew that he was up to no good." Olaf answers the settler.

The settler continues "Why don't we dis -fellowship the three families in question right away so that we do not have their poisonous tongues among us. They are bound to make problem for us."

Olaf answer "Please let them stay with us for a while and see how they conduct themselves, they are my flesh and blood."

"Then they should make obedience to Thorhilde after the coming crowning ceremony." The man continues and the rest of the settlers applaud.

Thorhilde addresses the settlers "I have taken upon me the important task of leading, guiding, counseling and helping you to a safe settlement in this choice land. Many times I have felt inadequate and weak but have been strengthened by my grandmother Gyda, many of you wonderful free men and women as well as the fantastic young men and women that have served as warriors for us. They have impressed me with their faith, courage and diligence in service, and I cannot think of any better young men and women on this very earth.

If any of them should want to marry a native, I surely side with Guttorm. Search the heart and mind of the young native. See if they are brave, diligent and have integrity before letting prejudice take control of your mind. I would like to see every one of you become educated and skilled, and to be diligent in keeping the commandments of the Lord. This settlement may become our heaven on earth, but only we can make it like that."

After Thorhilde had spoken, Guttorms continuous, "What is of importance to us now is how we plan and conduct our future. I propose that we recite the crowning ceremony for Thorhilde, but only after that we have invited the Shawnee Chief and his guard and family to attend. Let us send for them immediately and then proceed with the crowning ceremony when they arrive. Their quarters are not far from here and they should be here in a couple of days.

I also propose that they who do not want to give her their obedience become dis-fellowshipped and find themselves somewhere else to settle. Further on I propose that after the reciting of the crowning ceremony and the oath of obedience, we proceed with first of all the securing of our settlement. We must protect our people and especially the children, but also our animals, seed and equipment from raiders and thieves.

Secondly we must sow and plant what we can and hope for a late winter so that our crops will ripe. Thirdly I want you to build me a large enough church to house all of you simultaneously so that we can worship God every Sunday.

May the lord bless you all my children!"

Thorhilde asks Olaf to meet with her and thanks him for his support for her and says. "I am so happy to have you with my side in this challenging time of ours. Sincerely I do not think that I could have had a more trustful friend then what you have been to me." She embraces him and leave.

Next day the settlement is bursting with activity. It seems that everybody was doing something to make things look nice. The very place that the crowning ceremony was to be held was decorated with flowers and the whole environment was gorgeous looking. They were on the top of a bluff close to the river and were surrounded by forest trees of all kinds. It was so beautiful that men could not have created it, but the Lord himself.

One morning the Shawnee Chief and his follower arrived and were greeted welcome by Thorhilde and Guttorm. The settlers had everything prepared and soon everyone had put on their best cloths and was at their best behavior. All warriors had shined their weapons, shields and helms to their best and the women had made ready for a fiesta after the ceremony.

Thorhilde came to the crowning ceremony dressed in her full regalia and was a sight for everyone to admire.

Guttorm said to her smilingly "You better watch it, maybe the Shawnee Chief want you for a wife."

"Then he better be wanting!" Thorhilde answered also in smiles.

Then the whole crowning ceremony was recited as it was done in the Northwestern Settlement of Greenland, and they were all stunned by its beauty. The Shawnee chief and his family were all pleased to watch and came forward to make obedience to her. This was not planned and it struck Thorhilde as lightening, but she kept her calm and dignity.

Later on their Assiniboine scout Odin told them that the Shawnee chief had pronounced her as the High Queen of the Shawnee Tribe. When asked by Thorhilde what that meant, he told her that she was now their formal head and was to lead them in warfare as well as to protect them and see to that they were housed and fed.

It came as a shock to her, and she said to herself that this is to put even more responsibilities on her, but she braced herself and said to her "I will request the help from the Lord to manage everything that will come in my way!"

After the Shawnees had departed, Guttorm asked them all to partake in a ceremony of giving obedience to Thorhilde as their Queen. He was hoping that they would all do, but all the three families refused, and the next they packed their belongings and took their animals with them and left upriver.

Thorhilde worried that they would join with the Erie Tribe and with them instigate an attack on their settlement. She foresaw a former future with warfare instigated by Bjarni,s family and his followers. She also knew that if she had called a Thing and asked for their family heads to be put to the sword, the Thing would probably have followed her request seeing the coming danger to the settlement. The children would have been spared but most probably would have been full of hatred towards her especially, and the settlers in generality.

She had mixed feeling about her decision to let the three families leave, but felt that there had been enough bloodshed among the settlers already. "Please my Lord, protect us against the three families and their hatred and bitterness towards us. Please also soften the hearts of the Iroquois Nation towards us. They could become a fearful enemy to us and drive both us and the Shawnee out of this prime land."

Next day she summons everyone and says "I am fearful that the three families have plans to join with the Erie Tribe to the northeast of us and to become blood brothers with them. For the time being there is no danger to us but the time will come when they will instigate a desire in the Erie Tribe to claim this area as their hunting grounds and we must be prepared to defend our self and also prepare for a future migration further west together with the Shawnee especially if all the Iroquois tribes comes at us at the same time, which I do not think that they will. The most warlike and dangerous of them are the Erie Tribe which is feared by all native tribes.

The Shawnees are now our brothers and sisters and will stay by us in any tribulation that may fall upon us, and I will allow and support any young man or young woman that so desire to marry a Shawnee, but please also consider their integrity and ask for both your own and their parents approval. You are here in this land as free people and may choose everything for your self but remember that sometimes love makes people blind and please do not make lust take command of your feelings.

I as your Queen invoke all the choice blessings that are within my power to be bestowed upon you in this prime land. It is important that we start to marry earlier than we are accustomed to in Greenland where the average marriage age for a man was thirty two and the average marriage age for a woman was twenty eight. At the age of eighteen you should be fully prepared for marriage given that you are properly educated and skilled. I am putting this forward now for all the heads of the households to consider the wisdom of, and I will bow down to the decision of a majority of you going against me in this sensitive matter. I feel that we need to increase in number as quickly as possible and by the help of parents and grandparents and where needed from me, it should work out well.

I especially want all of us to be trained in combat and to be well armed and to live in fortified settlements due to an eventual attack by the dangerous Iroquois. We will work on this continually in order to always become stronger and more productive and safer.

Guttorm has asked for us to build him a church that is large enough to house all of us simultaneously. I feel that we shall first build a very large round structure that will both be a church as well as a cultural hall. This structure we will build in stone and turf so that any raiders cannot torch it. It will serve many purposes. First it will be a church and a cultural hall, but it will also be a fortress and a shelter in warfare. For that purpose we must make it so large that it also can accommodate our animals. Furthermore we can use it as a place to educate and skill us. We will also build four towers adjacent to it to support it as well as to be on lookout and to guard us. The towers will be built of stone and only have access from inside the big building, and will be manned by archers.

But I have one more project that I am also putting forward to you. This project will be time consuming but I still feel that we shall start that too after that we have finished the larger church and cultural hall. In Norway were our ancestors live for five hundred years, they started after the country became christened, to build wooden churches called Stav churches. We have with us one man that has taken part in such a construction in Norway, and he is willing to supervise us in a construction of the first Stav church in Vinland. Can you please come forward Inge and explain to us what we have to do in order for us to have it built here."

Before Inge has time to reply, one of the settlers asks "When are we to settle on our new farms Thorhilde?"

"This first winter I feel that we must stay close together in order to find our footing in this new land of our. Early next spring should be a good time to start dividing out lots for the new farms, but we must do so in agreement with the Shawnee, it is their hunting grounds."

"Aren't you their High Queen now?" another settler asked.

"Yes I am, but that does not mean that I can do everything that I want without counseling with the Shawnee Nation."

Inge comes forward and says" I have been so lucky that I have been a part of a construction team to completely finish a Norwegian Stav church. I will be happy to supervise the complete construction of a church here and will here tell you the main features of the building and what we need for it.

A Stav can be compared to the mast on "The Dragon of Greenland" but much larger. We need four very large and straight pine trunks to make the four corners of the main assembly room. These four pine trunks will be the backbone of the building. We will further more need some smaller pine trunks to carry the adjacent rooms to the main assembly room, the weapon house and the sacristy. The four large pine trees were in Norway chosen from the north side of a hill where they had been growing slowly for a very long time. They had also to be absolutely straight and without any faults. As a foundation for the four main Stavs they dug four large holes in the grounds where they were to stand. It had to be deeper than any extreme ground frost, and at the bottom of the hole, they put a large flat stone.

The pine trunk or Stav was first tarred where it was to be underground and raised. To avoid any contact with earth they jammed the trunk tight, firstly with large stones and then completely filled it up the remaining space with smaller stones in order to avoid rot. The rest of the building was then a matter of building onto the trunks. Roofing was all shingles and the finishing of both the outside and the inside was left to artistic wood crafters."

He continues "In Norway they often decorated their Stav churches with dragonheads on the outside and beautiful painted and carved pictures from the life of Jesus inside the church. Especially the altarpiece and the pulpit were highly decorated. The dragon heads on the outside were to scare evil spirits away from the church. Before anyone could enter the church they had to leave all weapons in the weapon house adjacent to the assembly hall before entering into the sanctity of the church itself. Some times the benches themselves were decorated. In Norway you can some times see names written of people of high standing or of people that have been working on it, often with only initials or their marks, if they were illiterate."

He continuous further "It will take years to finish it completely and I should like to hear from you how you fell about the project before I start to look for the construction material. Who are in favor of this large project?"

The response from the settlers is overwhelming positive and Inge, Thorhilde and especially Guttorm are all very pleased to hear it.

Thorhilde speaks again "I want to send expeditions all around this very continent to explore and chart it, and will myself lead one of them. We must acquire as much knowledge as we can quickly in order to progress and to survive. I have asked Guttorm and his assistant Baard to be the leaders of the settlement in my absence. They are both good men and will guide you and advice in that what is right and good for you. However you yourself are responsible for making the right decisions in your life.

Now I put before you a proposal "I propose that the expeditions shall consist of an equal amount of young unmarried men and woman. If any of them want to marry during the expeditions, I propose that they do so, but I will not send any off without their parents consent to do so. Think about it. I want them to be all above the age of eighteen. Also I want any man that sleeps with a woman on the expedition to marry her. If any of them after that are unfaithful to their partners, they will become dis- fellowshipped and have to leave the expedition wherever the expedition may be. Is this fair enough?"

The settlers are united in their response "Yes Thorhilde, this is but fare to any transgressor."

Thorhilde continues "Do not feel that you have to be married if you do not like anyone enough to make a partnership. There is still time for finding a partner when you return home again. I expect each expedition back home again by early fall next year."

Eric, an elderly and very experienced sailor, asks to see Thorhilde and caution her: "There is a very Old Norwegian saying that: it will bring bad luck if you bring women onboard a ship unless they travel; as passengers."

"That is only Old Norwegian superstition!" Thorhilde exclaim in surprise. "How can you that are so experienced and such a sober man believe in it?"

"My Queen, there have been so many sad stories being told by sailors that haven proven the opposite. I do not want neither my wife nor my daughters or grand daughters onboard any ship unless they have to travel as passengers."

Thorhilde is stunned and silent but understand that his feelings are definite.

"I will still sail with half men and half women", she informs Eric and leave him.

Thorhilde goes to bed early completely exhausted by all the events that have taken place in her fairly young life. The next day she spends with her foster daughter Singing Grass. Thorhilde tells her very gently that she has to be away for a year and that she Singing Grass will stay with Guttorm and his wife for that time. Guttorm and his wife are good people and will be looking well after you, but do not forget that you are my daughter!"

Singing Grass smiles and she understands that Thorhilde is emphasizing that she is not to be traded away to Guttorm and his wife. She smiles and says "I know that you love me mother and that you are not going to leave me ever, but please look after yourself too! There is only one Thorhilde!"

Thorhilde becomes so touched that she cannot stop the tears from coming. She hugs the little Blackfoot girl and rocks her back and forth. "Singing Grass and Thorhilde will always be together" she whispers in the little girl's ear.

"Even on the eternal hunting grounds mother?"

"Yes darling, even on the eternal hunting grounds!"

"Do you know mother that the awful marks that I had on my legs are almost gone do to the ointment that you applied to them. Now the other children are not teasing me anymore."

"Odin was the one who showed me how to find the plants I needed and how to make it. You should thank him too!"

"That I have already done "Bleeding Heart", but you are the one that have nursed me back to becoming like the other children."

"I am so happy darling that you are feeling accepted by the other children. You know darling Singing Grass that children can be very cruel to each others. Are there any children among us that are being taunted and ridiculed now?"

"There is on boy that they say are stupid. He always gets the blame for everything that is wrong and is often being beaten by the other boys. The girls ridicule him and think it is funny to watch."

"I will speak to their parents. Thank you for telling me!" Thorhilde is upset of what Singing Grass has told her.

Thorhilde summons the parents of the smaller children and ask for their support in stopping the mobbing of the little boy.

They are not all that cooperative and one of them says "We have always let the children manage their own affairs and feel that they are quite capable of sorting out their differences without any interference from the parents."

"It might seem fair to large and well established families that have many children to back them up if they should come in trouble, but is grossly unfair to lonely children without a net of supporting children around them." Thorhilde is upset and it is recognized by the parents.

"So is life, it is not always fair to us. That little boy is not the only one in this settlement that is having problems!" She is hard in her voice and it shakes Thorhilde.

Thorhilde is however not going to give in easily and she says "I am your elected Queen and you have all sworn obedience to me. This little boy that is now being ridiculed by your children is not my offspring but I feel it my responsibility to interfere in this matter and I ask you as your Queen and leader again to restrain your children from beating, taunting and ridiculing him?"

One of the women answers her sarcastically "Have you really any authority to intervene in such a matter?"

Thorhilde answers "Yes I have. I have promised to lead, guide and protect every one of you and that includes this little helpless child as well!"

They can all see that she is becoming angry and are weighing their answers. One of the men answers quietly "We all love and respect you Thorhilde but feel that you are overstepping your limit of authority in this matter!"

"So let me address you as a fellow Christian, if this had been your child, how would you then have reacted?" She has now regained control of herself.

The men and women become silent and leave quietly.

Thorhilde is so upset by their response that for a while she has problems in breathing properly, and she goes and sees Guttorm to have his response to it.

He hears her out and takes her down to the river. There he picks up a few stones and says "Look at these stones. They are now for a little while still wet on the outside, but they are still completely dry on the inside even though they have been lying in the Ohio River for thousand of years. The water has not managed to penetrate the inside of these stones. There are however stones that are penetrated by the river, but the large majority are not. So it is with the heart of men. Christianity has been with us for more than a thousand of years but have still only penetrated very few hearts.

You heart Thorhilde has become penetrated by Christianity, and your heart may be likened to the stones found in the river bed, that are penetrated by water. Hearts of men are unfortunately not easily softened. I am so happy that the settlers have chosen you as their Queen. You have all the qualities of a righteous sovereign. I will try to speak to the parents of the children, and even interfere if I must. We cannot have tings like this happen in our midst as Christians. It is far more important that we do interfere as adults to stop ridiculing of especially children than to build beautiful churches."

Thorhilde thanks him for his support and goes to rest. She is utterly exhausted and sleeps for a vey long time. During her sleep she dreams that she is meeting her family again and for a while she wanders if she has really been on the other side. She felt like that Gyda was coming to her in the dream and was warning her of something that was to happen to her. It was like she was wounded by something that had penetrated her coat of mail. She was first very upset but managed to push it away and remain her calm. First she thought of seeing Guttorm and tell him about the dream but pushed the thought away. Maybe he will think that

I have started seeing things, and that I am now longer in control, she thought to herself. I have been overworked and everything can possibly be explained in a rational way, and she left it like that.

She knew that she had to prepare for their expeditions and she had a long conversation with Odin in a broken Siouan/Norse language. Odin had picked up a lot of Norse words and expressions on the journey and was very well aware of the meaning of most of what was said. Also she understood that if Odin came to the full knowledge of their Norse language, the settlers would not any more bother to try to learn Siouan. She decided there and then that as soon as the church and cultural hall was finished that they were to start language classes in both Siouan and Algonquian languages.

Thorhilde asked Odin what he thought of the place that they had chosen for a settlement and he answered that he thought that the place had good hunting grounds and that the soil was fertile and would yield good crops. Also there are plenty of forests and good water.

Asked what he thought of the brotherhood with the Shawnee he shrugged his shoulders and said "They are good and fearful warriors and will be true friends to you but they are lazy and thieving when it suits them. Be alert against them too and they do not treat their wives well."

It was obvious that Odin was prejudiced against them so Thorhilde wasn't to sure where the whole truth and nothing but the truth was. However she knew she had to be on her guard against the Shawnee as well.

She asked Odin to tell her about everything that he knew about the neighboring tribes.

Odin answers "To the northeast of us are the hunting grounds of a very warlike and ferocious tribe, the Erie. They will let their women torture a captured enemy to either death or their acceptance of bravery. If they think that he proved himself in either battle or during torture they can ask to have him as their husband. They have a matriarchal society where the female lineage is the important one, and their kings are always from the female lineage. They are also cannibals. You better not be taken prisoner by one of them.

To the east of them living on the shores of the Finger Lakes are the Senecas, Cayugas, Oneidas and Onondagas and shortly further east on the Mohawk River are the Mohawks. Those five tribes are together the most fearful enemy you can encounter. They have the same social system as the Erie Tribe but are not in fellowship with them.

On the northern side of Lake Erie and of Lake Ontario are the hunting grounds of the Huron Nation and the Wyandot Nation. They are also Iroquoian, and together with the Erie, Seneca, Cayuga, Oneida, Onondagas, Mohawks and Cherokees members of the Iroquoian language family."

"Do you understand their language?" Thorhilde interrupts him.

"I understand the meaning of their words.' Odin answered and continued. "To the southeast of you where you are now, are the hunting grounds of the Cherokee nation. They have migrated south from further northeast and have tradition of mixing with white people that probably are settlers from the Southern Settlement of Greenland, from what you have told me earlier. Cherokees are the friendliest of the Iroquoian speaking nations and you will probably meet some of during your travel on the continent."

"Tell me about the Shawnee and their fellow tribes." Thorhilde asked Odin.

"The Shawnee is a large tribe with hunting grounds on both sides of the Ohio River. The name Shawnee means Southerners. They are closely related to the Delaware Nation that lives by the large ocean to the east. Shawnees are member of the Algonquian language family which is also spoken by the Blackfoot Nation, the Cheyenne Nation and the Arapaho Nation on the Northwest Plains, and also by the Fox Nation, the Sauk Nation, the Ottawa Nation, the Chippewa Nation and the Cree Nation further north."

"What language does the Mandan's speak?" Thorhilde questions.

"Beside the three Sioux Nations, the Nakota Sioux or Assiniboine, the Dakota Sioux and the Lakota Sioux or Teton Sioux, the Mandan Nation and their neighbors the Hidatsa Nation as well as the Crow Nation and the Kansa Nation are Siouan speaking. The Ho Chunk Nation of Wisconsin is also Siouan speaking."

"Tell me what you now about the Mandan Nation Odin?"

"Hundreds of years earlier the Mandan Nation lived by the Ohio River. They came very early in contact with traders and hunters from Greenland and they intermixed with them.

It has been told me that they have legends of Christianity similar to the creation of the world that you have. They must have learned that from a Christian people and most likely from your people in Greenland. They are very light skinned and look fare more like your people than any native tribe that I know of.

Legend says that they have been on a three hundred years migration from the Ohio River Valley unto where they are now in the Upper Missouri Valley. Also they do not build their villages the native way of spreading out, but rather the Viking way as I have seen you do, and have also been told, rather built around an open square in the center. Are we going to visit with them?"

"I hope so Odin!" Thorhilde proclaimed with gladness in her voice. "Do you think that we will manage to get the largest ship that far up the river?"

"If we drag it overland passed the rapids yes" Odin answered.

Thorhilde now are feeling that she has sufficient information enough to plan for the exploring expeditions. She wants them to start as soon as possible and she summons the settler once more.

She says "I want us to during this coming year to start three expeditions as soon as possible. I will personally lead one expedition in "The Dragon of Greenland". We will leave in two days and I will need fifty unmarried men above eighteen years of age and fifty young women above eighteen years of age to come with me for a short year. Have you young unmarried girls heard the stories of the Scythian Amazons?"

They answers "No we have not heard about the Scythian Amazons"

Thorhilde explains "Gyda told me about them when I was young. The Scythians that are among our ancestors were the first to use women on the battlefield. They were feared by their enemies for their bravery. May you become like them."

The young girls clapped their hands in joy." I want to join. Please let me come with you."

Thorhilde continued "There will be room for every unmarried man and every unmarried woman above the age of eighteen in one of the ships. I will also have with me at least four experienced sailors to manage the ship in open sea. We are first to explore the Mississippi River right down to the ocean. From there we are to explore the eastern coastline of Vinland right up to where the Iroquois River empties into the ocean. When the river is free of ice we will row it up the rive and drag it past the Niagara falls into the Lake Erie and back home again over Lake Huron, Lake Michigan, Chicago River, Illinois River and back on to

Mississippi River and Ohio River. Coming home again I will like to be a part of the allotment of farms together with the Shawnee Chief, so that we have the chief's approval.

Furthermore I want the two vey small ships that we have, the trading ship and the hunting ship to go on a very long and also perhaps dangerous journey. I want also these ships crewed with half unmarried men and unmarried women above the age of eighteen. Both these two ships will have four experienced sailors onboard. These two ships are to explore the Missouri river as far as they can, and also to find a passage in the mountains where they can drag their ships over the continental divide and down to Snake River and further on to the Western Ocean. Try to find Shoshone scouts for the crossing of the continental divide. There must be an opening somewhere in the mountains. From there you will journey home past the Aleutian Islands and north of this continent until you reach Helluland and the same route back as that we have travelled now.

These ships are about thirty feet long and are equipped with eight pair of oars and also with sails. They are sturdy built and can manage creeks, land and ocean passages. We will need fifteen men and fifteen women onboard each of these small ships making each of them crewed with thirty-four altogether. I want only physically very strong men and woman onboard these ships. They will have to a lot of dragging and pushing.

Thirdly I want some smaller ships to explore the Ohio River as far as possible and then drag them overland across the gap leading to the Potomac River and from there to the ocean.as Further explore the Delaware River with its tributaries, before turning home again. We all need food, weapons and gifts for the natives in our way. Before we leave in a couple of days we will ask Guttorm to bless us.

Chapter X

Explorations across the continent – 1330-31

"The Dragon of Greenland" is ready to leave and so are the other ships as well. The settlement is bustling with excitement, and most excited are the young and unmarried men and women that are to partake in this adventurous voyage.

Their families did not try to stop them from parting, when they saw the joy and excitement in their faces. They wished them all good luck and were happy for them. All of them did partake of the communion before they left and were blessed by Guttorm.

Provisions were onboard of everything that they were in need of for a whole year both of summer and winter clothing and any thinkable needed equipment was brought onboard. They were very well clear of the need for fishing and hunting equipment as well as small gifts to give and to trade with the natives that they were to meet.

They followed the stream down the Ohio River and had plenty of time to admire the beauty of the land. Torhilde had divided the ship into two sections, the most forward was to be for the men and the aftermost was to be for women. She had the men and the four experienced sailors handle the sails but let the girls manage the steering of the ship under the guidance of two of the experienced sailors. Thorhilde also set the women to the oars when the ship had to be rowed.

"It is good for you to know everything that is necessary in the handling of a ship she told them. First you will learn to row and to steer the ship, and later on you can learn how to manage the sail and to tie knots and anything else that is necessary to know."

The young women smiled and thought life was fantastic.

Thorhilde had told them that they were to visit the Tennessee River settlement before they ventured southward on the Mississippi River. Just before nightfall they reached the Tennessee River and Thorhilde ordered the ship to anchor in the river for the night. "The Rivers that we are to sail on this voyage are often dangerous to navigate do to strong and sudden under streams and moving sandbanks. A few times we will probably ram the bottom of the ship on one of these sand banks, but do not let that worry you, we will come afloat again."

The ships crew went early to bed but for two watchmen, one at the bow and one at the aft of the ship. Before they lay down to sleep, Thorhilde asked them to sleep on their sword and close to their bows and arrows.

During the night many strange noises were heard and Thorhilde awakened several times and wondered if they were natives that were signaling to each others. They were now outside Shawnee land, and on the north bank of the Ohio River were the hunting grounds of the Illinois Nation, and on the south bank of the Ohio River were the hunting grounds of the Chickasaw Nation.

When morning came Thorhilde led them in prayer and asked for the protection of the Lord for them and for their families and friends. After that they had breakfast and done with that lifted anchor and started rowing upstream the Tennessse River.

Before nightfall they came to a settlement that had to be of Nordic origin. It was derelict looking and the settlers looked to be an unhappy lot. There were no light in their eyes like as if they had lost all hope of a good future. They all came to meet them some fifty of them. They told them that their grand parents had settled here many years earlier but things had not worked out well for them. When they were told of the new settlement to the north in Shawnee land, their eyes seemed to catch glimmers of hope.

When they were told the whole story about the abandonment of the Northwestern Settlement of Greenland and the reason for it, they nodded in admiration for the decision to leave.

"Can we come and stay with you in your settlement" they asked and Thorhilde immediately answered "When we leave here, we will immediately return upstream the Ohio River and send ships down here to bring you and your families home to us. Are you being threatened by the Chickasaw Nation?"

"They answered no, but they are not good neighbors. We have been thieved of most of our animals and most of our equipment"

Thorhilde says "I propose that I return home immediately with as much cargo as we can take and then return back with sufficient many ships to evacuate all of you in a couple of days. Let us start to load onboard your most precious positions."

To her surprise they managed to get all of the families, animals and tools onboard "The Dragon of Greenland" in the short time before nightfall.

Thorhilde ordered the ship to be turned around and to drift with the stream hoping not to be grounded on a sand bank during the night. She had an uneasy feeling with staying at the settlement during nightfall. It was something creepy with the place.

She ordered complete silence and darkness during the slow drift downstream. Have all animals lie down and tie them closely so that they do not stampede, and be ready for arrows to come. All the four experienced sailors were maneuvering the ship now and things seemed to be safe.

Then they suddenly heard some horrible screams from the shore and a shower of arrows suddenly came at them from a very close bank to the north. However the crew was prepared and ducts the arrows with their shields. Now it was the Vikings time to return fire. They had trained archers and could dimly see movements of many people between the trees on the north bank.

"Fire your arrows when you are ready!" Thorhilde ordered and soon they cool hear screams from people being hit. This however did not stop them from following the ship and trying again and again to ram them with their arrows.

At one point the river was very narrow and there were tall trees close by where assassins could hide, and simultaneously they could feel the ship lightly touching the bottom of the Tennessee River. Thorhilde almost felt her heart up in her throat and prayed to the Lord. "Please Lord; do not let us ground now."

She shouted to the men onboard to make a tortoise with the shields to cover both you and your animals, as we pass through this narrow and dangerous narrow pass of the river. Luckily the sailor steering the ship had on a coat of mail and a full helmet that kept him safe, while the rest of them duct under the tortoise of shields.

During the narrow passage they several times felt the ship keel plow the river sandbanks but always came loose again in time to regain steering control. As they were showered with arrows, miraculously none of the men, women or animals was hurt. Tennesse River broadened and the ship eventually reached the Ohio River just in time for daylight to arrive.

An old sailor warned Thorhilde "On the river banks of the Ohio River to the east and south of us there are still dangers to come. It is Chickasaw hunting grounds for a good portion of a days rowing and there is especially one place that is dangerous where the river makes a sharp turn and is narrower and faster. The point we have to turn have high bluffs covered with high trees and brush. It is and ideal place for an ambush. I bet they are waiting for us to do us harm."

"What is you advice Eric?" she asked the old sailor.

"It will take us at least five hours to reach that point. Why don't we row on as fast as we can and then proceed the same way as we did in the narrow pass? Make a tortoise and stay covered. Your archers will not be able to reach them; they will be too high up."

"But who will row the ship? They will shoot at the oarsmen!" Thorhilde was bewildered.

"How many coats of mails do you have onboard Thorhilde?"

"We have ten coat of mails of good quality onboard Eric. Will that be enough?" Thorhilde answers him.

"It will have to do us. I propose that you let ten fit oars men put on coats of mails and spread them out five on each side of the ship and have them do as I did when the arrows came flying, turn their heads away from the direction of the arrows. Let everybody keep on rowing at full speed until you hear their war cry. Then quickly make a tortoise and hide. Torhilde pass on this information to everyone onboard and asks them to be prepared.

Around noon they are approaching the dangerous place and they are all trying to look at ease in order to surprise the assassins. Suddenly some horrible shrieks penetrate the air and Thorhilde shouts "Under the tortoise fast." Not long after a shower of arrows flies through the air and mostly hits the shields. A few of the oarsmen gets hit but none of the arrows penetrates their coat of mails that are made of chains of rings.

"The Dragon of Greenland "is rowed slowly but steadily around the dangerous point in the turn of the Ohio River and not long after, they are in safe waters. It was like their attackers were too sure that they were to harm them and that they lost heart when they did not succeed. After rowing as far as to be in Shawnee land on both riverbanks they anchor for the night and rest. They keep very sharp lookout though and are ready for everything.

They are surprising everyone with their speedy return and the Tennessee River settlers are made very welcome by them all. The crew rest one day and Thorhilde questions every one of them if they want to stay onboard for the continuing voyage and not even one of them opts out.

Downstream Ohio River they are now very cautious and are on sharp lookout where dangers might be. Thorhilde takes the advice from the old sailor Eric, and asks him to point out where dangers might be. Any suspicious sound or a good place for an ambush has the full crew on high alert. After a couple of days easing slowly downriver they are in the Mississippi River proper.

"Here we will be safe from sudden attacks Eric tells Thorhilde. The only dangers here will be when we go ashore for hunting or for fresh clean water, or we may strike a sandbank and have to maneuver our ship afloat again."

"But are we not in a river full of fresh water Eric?" Thorhilde asks him.

"I would not drink the water from the Mississippi River. It is muddy and do not taste good. It is probably not dangerous to drink though."

"Where do you advise us to stop for fresh water and for hunting?"

"If we let the ships drift with the stream a couple of more days and nights, we will have the hunting grounds of the Caddo Nation on our west bank of the Missisipi River. They will be friendly to us and we can trade some of our small gifts for fresh water, meat, fruits and berries. On the east bank of the river are the hunting grounds of the Chickasaw Nation. Them we have met earlier."

"The Dragon of Greenland" made a several days stop at a Caddo village near where the junction of the Arkansas River and the Mississippi

River. They were very friendly to the Vikings and they traded the necessities that they needed with them in a quiet harmony of mutual friendship. After a short week of resting they continued southward towards the sea for several days and eventually entered into a region that was completely new to everyone, but for Eric who had been there earlier on a trading ship.

Now there were strange new trees to be seen and the air was warm and humid and there seemed to be insects everywhere. The Mississippi River had now become broad and majestic, swelling up and becoming fatter and fatter by all its nourishments from all its children, grandchildren and great grandchildren.

Eric told them that the Natchez Nation had their hunting grounds here. They also farm this land and raise maize, beans and squash for food supplement. They are an industrious native tribe he told us. "The Dragon of Greenland" stopped with the Natchez Natives for several weeks in order to study their habits and food culture.

Thorhilde had started becoming very good friends with Olaf. Since he was one of her personal guards, he was always close to her, as was the other five guards too. If she went for short walks, she always brought at least one of our guards with her, and it often happened to be Olaf. She could not see anything wrong in it and so did not anybody else onboard. They all knew of what happened to his parents.

The voyage further south the Mississippi River takes them through a swampy area full of strange looking birds that Eric says are pelicans. They are native birds of this area and are as plentiful as you can imagine. The Mississippi River snakes itself towards the ocean and when "The Dragon of Greenland" eventually enter the wide open ocean, they all know that they have been entertained by the most fantastic Lady of the World, the majestic Mississippi River. The ocean to the south of the Mississippi River is both warm and humid and as they steer east in order to return north again they see a very low swampy coastline in the far horizon.

Since this is new areas to them, Thorhilde orders them to only proceed in daylight to be certain to avoid dangerous situations. Eric tells them of some horrible storms that some times sweeps over these areas. They are circular storms that rotate around a center unlike ordinary winds that are blowing more permanently in one direction.

He tells them that if they should ever encounter one of these storms, they would better be out at the open sea rather than close to the coastline. The wind is of horrible magnitudes and in a very short time whisk up high and freak waves that are capable of lifting any ship high up and throw them inland as easy as can be.

"How can we now that such a storm is coming?" Thorhilde asks.

"Firstly, any storms in this area that we are to sail in now are that kind of storm. They are made from the very warm water that comes up to us from further south and from Africa itself. An indication is often a complete calm and rising water. Rising water may be noticed at shore but out at sea, an experienced sailor may sense that something is coming. The natives of the islands have this built in indicator that warns them of these storms beforehand. If I get a feeling of a coming storm, I will warn you and we must try to be on the open sea and rig down everything that the wind can take hold of. Take down sail and mast and if possible also take down the dragonhead before it disappears overboard. You can re-erect it later. Lay down on the deck as flat as you can and put your shields on top of you to protect you against torrential rain. If the ships fill up with water we must start to bail it out at any cost."

They sailed around the large peninsula that consisted mainly of flat and swampy land on the western part of it, but more sandy beaches on the eastern side of it. Eventually they came to a little natural good port on the eastern side of the peninsula and stayed there for some time and rested.

A day or two after they had put to sea and was all happily sailing northward along the eastern coastline of Vinland, Eric started to get that funny feeling of that something was far wrong. He became very silent and started to look very curiously southward as he was expecting an enemy or something strange event to happen and Thorhilde approached him and asked

"Are you suspecting a tropical storm Eric?"

He looked at her very serious and said "I am not a hundred percent sure. But there is definitely building up to something to the south of us and it s coming our way. Can we sail further out into the ocean to be in open sea if a storm hits us?"

"Of course we can." Thorhilde answered him and ordered them to sail straight east out from the mainland. Very soon the mainland of

Vinland disappeared from their eyes and they were in open waters. Now they all could sense that something was coming their way and that very fast too. The sky was already becoming very dark and there were rapid movements of the clouds.

Eric became very serious and clear and distinct. "Let us immediately saw down both the two stems of the ship and secure them before the wind gets hold of them. Take the forward one with the dragonhead first. It is the most dangerous. Immediately lower sail, take the wedges that hold the mast off, and lay the mast down. Secure it properly with ropes before the wind take hold of it. We can row the ship meantime until we can restore it. Stow the stem parts, sail and steering oar under the thwarts of the ship, as well as all oars.

Act fast, the storm is coming flying at us!" Eric shouts out. He helps to lower the sail, and is not a second too early; some fierce wind gusts have already reached them. Then he shouts out again "Secure the steering oar immediately. Loosen it and bring it under the thwarts together with the oars."

The crew just managed to cut down the two skip stems before some horrible wind gusts sweeps over them. To loosen the steering oar and bring it onboard take the full power of the men to handle. They just manage to get in inboard and undamaged before the storm is over them.

Eric shouts to them "See to that everything is properly secured!"

Then he shouts again, but can barely be heard "All of you lay flat down on the deck with the shields on top of you. See to that the shields are jammed under the thwarts as well to stop the wind from getting hold of them."

They all barely managed to fulfill his last instruction before the very full fury of the storm is over them. "It isn't so much the waves that is dangerous to us here out in the open sea, bur the wind. It has such a ferocity that it can take a man that is foolish enough to stand up straight and throw him like a ball far away in seconds. Do not even try to crawl against the wind." Eric shouts to them. The crew follows his instruction fully and after a couple of hours the winds tapers off and the sea has regained its calm again.

After the storm has disappeared further north, Thorhilde asks them all to kneel down and thank the Lord for having shielded them throughout this ordeal.

"The Dragon of Greenland" did not look like a dragon anymore but more like a plucked hen. But the crew didn't care. They were as happy as could be and took to the oars with songs in their hearts and with smiles on their faces. Thorhilde was watching them and became filled with warmth and gratitude towards the Lord and towards her young crew.

She ordered the ship to be rowed towards the shore and to search out a good harbor to do the repair work in. They soon found a good harbor and tied up the ship and rested after having put out guards for the night.

The next morning they were surrounded by natives that looked more curious than hostile, and Eric told Thorhilde that they were Creek Natives. The Creek Nation has its hunting grounds in this area of Vinland. They have been in contact with trading ships before and will be friendly towards us. Give them some small gifts and they will be happy as children.

Thorhilde asked to be dressed in her royal regalia before she went ashore to meet with them. Odin had advised her to do so. They will only respect you highly if they think you are a prominent person. Being dressed in full regalia is one way of showing your position. She also asked her men to be armed and ready for a sudden outburst of violence, should it so happen.

Two of the young men brought with them some small gifts that she offered them and they beckoned to and elderly man that had just arrived.

Thorhilde thought immediately that he must be one of their Chiefs and went slowly towards him in order to greet him whereupon his guards immediately shielded him and pointed their spears towards her. She understood that they thought that she might wanted to attack him and stopped calmly and beckoned to them that they had come as friends. The natives seemed to be uncertain of what to do and suddenly they all disappeared.

Thorhilde asked Eric what he thought they should do, and he answered that they were a friendly nation but that they had been attacked by northern tribes, and maybe also attacked from the sea, what might explained why they were suspicious. She knew that she had to make a decision very fast. If they were to depart in fear of an attack by perhaps thousands of warriors, they should better depart immediately before they could assemble their warriors. But somehow she didn't feel any fear either and she decided to wait. She told her crew to be ready to leave immediately by any sign of hostility from ashore.

As the day went by and nothing happened, she was about to order a retreat out in the open sea when suddenly they could hear drums. It was not like the sound of war drums but more like musical drums and it did not frighten them at all. After a little while a procession of people arrived at the beach and this time Thorhilde was sure that this was a Creek king.

He was dressed in impressive robes and was surrounded by servants of both sexes, but seemingly without any armed bodyguard. The procession came close to the ship and he beckoned to Thorhilde to come ashore and meet him.

She took her personal guard along, and also the two young men with the small gifts. When she came within ten feet of him she stopped and beckoned to him that she had brought gifts for him, whereupon he smiled and thanked her. He beckoned for her to come closer to him and he was openly admiring her beauty. Before he said anything he came forward and touched her red blond hair and showed it to his wife in openly admiration. The women that were following him came now forward and touch her clothes and skin and smiled happily like they had touched some Godly being.

Her guard was watching in stunned silence not really knowing what to do. Thorhilde smiled to them and beckoned that she was alright.

The king asked if he could see the ship and was escorted onboard. Erick that understood a few words of their Muskogean language tried as best he could to tell him that they had to cut both the stems and the mast in order to avoid the wind blow them away. When he sees the dragon head, he becomes exited and asks if he can have it as a gift. The men look at Thorhilde and she knows that she has to make a decision. She takes the dragon head and places it loose on the fore stem of the ship to show the Creek King where it should have been and he nods that he understands well. But then he beckons to her "The dragon head is not where it should have been. It has left its place for the obvious reason to go somewhere else, and that is to my house"

Thorhilde understands that in order to gain their friendship and help, she has to give in. She can have a new dragonhead made when she comes home, and she takes the dragonhead and gives it to him in a way that he understands it is a present. When she sees his gladness and thankfulness she immediately feels no remorse for what she did. She knows now that this will secure her crew and ship, and that is her duty. The king then beckons, and asks her and her guard to come to his house and eat with them. She sends message to her crew to stay alert and ready onboard while she and her guard are to be entertained by the king.

Thorhilde and her guards were escorted to a larger village not too far away and treaded in the most reverent way by their host. She understood that he was sincere in his friendship with them and wanted to do her outmost to secure his help in getting their ship back in a seaworthy condition. They are all treated to dishes of maize bread, stewed beans, squash and poultry. To drink they are getting something that is unrecognizable to them, but is however tasty. Everyone seems to be in a good mode and the king now as well wants to give them a choice present. He claps his hands and in comes a beautiful looking very young girl that he obviously wants to give to one of the young guardsmen as a wife.

Thorhilde is first astounded by the proposal but then regain control of her and smiles. She turns to her guard and asks smilingly "How about having the girl make the choice of her husband? Will you all stand by me in my decision?"

All the six guardsmen smiles and say "Yes, we will stand by you!"

Thorhilde point to herself and says Thorhilde, and then ask her for her name. The little girl answers Talisa, and her father indicates in sign language that the name means Beautiful Water.

Then Thorhilde beckons to all her guardsmen indicating that Talisa has the choice of either of them before she make the choice of whom she wants for her husband, before she take the little and very young girl gently by her hand and present her one by one to every one of her young guardsmen by name.

"This is Gunnar, please meet Talisa!" he is the first one to be presented to her. Thorhilde feel immediately love between the two of them, but continues to present all of her young guardsmen to Talisa. She then points to all of them and asks Talisa with a big smile on her face to make a choice of one of them.

Talisa giggles a little before she goes straight over to Gunnar and places her self next to him. Everyone in the room shouts with joy and the King makes clear indications to that he wants a marriage ceremony started immediately in the village.

Thorhilde wants most of her crew present and asks for them to be sent for. She tells one of her guards to run back to the ship and have they all come armed as fast as they can, to celebrate the wedding with them. Only have the sailors but Eric, stay back and see to the ship. She knew that darkness would soon come; but noticed that the natives were preparing large stockpiles of firewood to last probably for the most of the night. They were all seated in a large circle with the bride and groom to be in the center waiting for the native ceremony to start. Everyone seemed excited and the atmosphere was electrifying. Thorhilde had Eric sitting next to her to interpret what he could interpret and to tell the meaning and symbolism of the ceremony.

Eric told Thorhilde that once that the couple was wed the native Creek way; she should perform a wedding the Christian and Viking way thereafter to completely legalize it.

"But do I have authority to do that?" she asked him.

"As the formal captain and commander in chief of us you do have that authority" he answered.

"But is that only valid if we are onboard a ship?"

"Generally speaking yes, but under very special circumstances dispensations from the law can be given." Eric answers her.

"Who have the authority to give such dispensations Eric?"

"You have, my Queen!" Eric says with a smile on his face and Thorhilde gave in to his eloquent reasoning.

"We will do that!" Thorhilde does agree fully now.

The native ceremony was a beautiful event to watch and after that is fully performed native dancers dressed in their traditional costumes performs for hours for them.

Thorhilde approaches the Creek King and beckones that she too wants to bless the couple the Christian Viking way. She trained herself beforehand to conduct a marriage onboard the ship if it should become needed, but she is still nervous that she shall make a mistake and say something wrong. Before the ceremony is to start, two young warrior couples that have been courting on the ship also comes forward and asks if she can perform a triple marriage so that they can legally stay together as married couples.

"Of course you can!" she says smilingly "Come and join us!"

The natives become exited when they understand that they are being a part of an historic event. They shout with joy and the atmosphere becomes almost hilarious.

She wants to use her own crown that she has with her and is carried in a small casket by one of her guards, but does not want to give that away. To avoid misunderstandings she let the native understand that the crown that she will put on her own head during the ceremony also will be put on the three brides only symbolically to beautify the ceremony. The Chief and his adviser's first seem somewhat confused but eventually take the point and nods in understanding.

Thorhilde conducts the wedding ceremony in dignity and with reverence and when Talisa nods for yes to marry Gunnar, Thorhilde takes the crown from her own head and gently places it on Talisas head. The ordinance is most beautiful and the natives shout of joy and admiration. Then she gently take the crown back and put it on her own head and perform two similar marriage ceremonies to the two Young Viking couples. After the ceremonies are over, Thorhilde keep the crown on her head in order to avoid misunderstandings by the natives.

It is getting late but before they are to end, Thorhilde asks if the young Warriors can perform a few Norwegian Folk Dances for the Creek audience. Willingly they line up and without any music but with song and dance performs to their best. The response from the natives is nothing but fantastic and the celebration continues into the early morning light. The wedded couples are all offered huts of their own and retreat quietly from the rest of the celebrating party earlier.

Everything seems now to work out well for the traveling party. They receive all the help that they need to repair the ship and are well fed and entertained by the Creek nation. When they are staying there, Thorhilde is approached by an additional six couples that want to marry, and the wedding ceremonies are recited the same way with much joy for everyone. All the twelve young men and women are smiling happily and enjoying life in general and their coming spouse in particular.

Thorhilde understands that the winters are fierce on the northeastern coast of Vinland and counsel with Eric on the wisdom of trying to navigate in these waters before the weather becomes better and they can sail in safety. "The Dragon of Greenland" has not been constructed for high ocean voyages, at least not in winter time.

She wanted to be back home early enough, to become become a part in the allotment of farms to the settlers. However she also see the need to navigate in safety. The tropical storm that they encountered is not forgotten easily.

Eric tells her that they can follow a warm stream in gentle and smooth waters, a good part of the way and in complete safety since the tropical storm season is over for this time. "However, I warn you of the northeastern coastal waters, the very cold waters from the East Greenland Stream sets down these waters and also carry icebergs. Weather conditions are often stormy and very unpredictable. I advise you to hibernate here in this tranquil region until at least comes April. Then you can visit the Cherokee Nation to the north of us and later the Powhatan Nation that has its hunting grounds west of the large bay even some further north. The weather conditions in the waters that we are to meet later on are so dangerous and unpredictable, that I propose we are extreme alert, and seek harbor immediately if the wind starts to increase."

Thorhilde thanks him for his advice and rely this to everyone which does not seem at all unhappy to stay longer at this beautiful place among all these friendly natives. The rest of the winter passes away under such happy circumstances that the crew of the ship feels like they are in paradise.

But April arrives and they are back to reality. Now they are making themselves ready to sail north, but not before a grand fiesta have been given to their honor. It takes place during most of the day and the night and both tears and laughter is shed among them before the final departure takes place.

They leave the friendly nation with sadness in their hearts but with joy when thinking of all the good time they had together.

Thorhilde makes a couple of days stop with the Cherokee nation a couple of days further north before continuing. They inhabit a beautiful area called "The Blue Ridge Mountains" and further out to the ocean. The Cherokee Nation are used to the Greenlanders from hundred of years back and have also intermixed with them to a degree that many of them are Nordic looking. They are very friendly and helpful to Thorhilde and her crew, but they are now becoming short of time and have to leave after only a few days stop.

She has been told by Eric that at a western point further north the warm stream that they are following suddenly meets with the very cold Greenland stream setting southward and that the temperature will drop dramatically in seconds of time.

"Do to the meeting of these two so complete different currents the weather is often stormy, or if calm, foggy." Eric then warns her again. "When we pass the dangerous headland, we have three options. We can proceed northward very close to the shore, sail further out at sea and avoid the southbound current or sail into the Chesepiooc Bay where the Powhatan Nation has their hunting grounds. The Powhatan Nation is Algonquian speaking, and the name Powhatan means a fall in a streaming river or, River Fall if you like that better. The name Chesepiooc is an Algonquian name for Great Waters, and is a very good explaining name for that great bay. There we can find refuge for stormy weather, if needed."

When the ship reaches the eastern point and suddenly encounters the cold southbound Greenland Stream the weather does not seem to be too bad and Thorhilde ask Eric to navigate as close to the shore as is safe.

They propel the ship by both sail and oars and progress fairly smoothly along the coastline. Eric tells them that the land they see are the ancient hunting grounds of the Delaware or as they are also called Lenape Nation. The next day they are clearly on the estuary of a great river and Eric tells them that the river is called the Delaware River after the Delaware Nation.

Delawares and Shawnees are blood brothers and Thorhilde hopes to get good reports from the one expedition that she sent to explore that region traveling upstream the Ohio River and then dragging their ship overland to the Potomac River and the Delaware River systems. Eric tells her that the Delaware Nation is very friendly towards strangers and those settlers and traders from the Southeastern Settlement of Greenland have been there often in the past.

They voyage further north along the coastline, and when the wind starts to increase they enter the first safe coastal entrance that arrives before them. A large bay open up before them and they become aware of that they are in the estuary of a large river.

Eric knows this river as well. The natives call this river Mahicantuck, meaning a river that flows two ways. This is due to the effect of the tide that pushes the tidewater up river and changes the direction of flow. Further north river is the hunting grounds of the Mohawk Nation.

The "Dragon of Greenland" is then rowed through a narrow sound to the east and eventually into a large sound or inlet that protects them from the fierce wind that they can hear hauling further out on the ocean. There they anchor for the night close to the shore and put out watches and sleep on their swords and bows.

Next day they are surrounded by natives from the Pequot Nation. They are surrounding the ship with their canoes and are first only looking very curiously at the ship but when Thorhilde sees that their attitude is changing, she orders the anchor weighed and the ship to proceed. With the help of sail and oars the Vikings are soon away from a coming danger. They can now see more canoes coming at them from both sides of the inlet, but to far away from them to be of any threats.

Eric tells them that the Pequot Nation is generally friendly but unpredictable. Their hunting grounds are on both the large island that is now sheltering them from the violent sea on our starboard side and also on the continent itself to our port side.

For their safety against attack from the Pequot Nation, they stay in the middle of the sound until it opens up and they can both see and hear the frowning ocean.

Thorhilde understands that as long as they stay where they are, they are both safe from the sea and the Pequot Nation. In their small canoes, they are not likely to venture that far out towards the ocean. However she orders the ship to be placed in a position of the sound that they are barely safe from either of the two dangers. She asks the crew to pray together with her and ask for their protection from both hostile natives and the violent seas.

The weather stays bad for weeks and they are getting both tired and soon they are short of both food and water. Thorhilde asks Eric of the danger of proceeding further north the next day.

He answers her. "We have a fairly good chance of rounding the outmost cape before darkness if we start very early and use both sail and oars the best we can. We ought to maneuver the ship to the inside of the two large islands that we can see in the horizon, and be ready for a dash around the cape itself the next day. We will take in some water and will need to both row and bail the best we can in order to prevail, but I do think that we will make it.

The day came and early that morning they started with full sails and everyone at the oars as well to gain momentum against the power of the sea. They reach a good speed and are in high spirit until they are ready to turn straight north. A strong northerly wind is blowing directly and strongly against them and the southbound Greenland Stream is also coming straight at them, makes them almost coming to a standstill.

Eric however is optimistic and asks them to stay so close to the shore that they are not met by the full effect of the southbound ocean stream. Furthermore he tells them that the wind will soon ease off, and continue rowing. After several hours of hard rowing the wind suddenly decreases fast and they make good progress.

During the rest of the day they have all given their outmost at the oars, and just before sunset they can see that the land is starting turning slightly westward and they can take the use of the sail again. Also they are out of the cold water stream. The ship is now safe and they thank the Lord for his help to keep them all preserved. Even if they were prepared for it, the ship did not take in water, but they labored at the oars, to a degree that almost all of them had large blisters in their hands. Especially the girls, where not at all happy about that.The night went by, and Thorhilde ordered the ship to drift slowly, so that they could all rest, but for the watches.

Coming ashore the next day they were welcomed by very friendly natives that Eric said were Wampanoag Nation. They were extremely helpful and friendly towards them and they stayed with them for about a week to gather strength and to wait for better weather. Food and water were given them plentiful in exchange of some small gifts, and the settlers left with thanks in their hearts to both the Lord and the Wampanoag nation for their mercy and help towards them.

While they were staying with the Wampanoag Nation, Thorhilde took some time of just to pull herself together. She went on several trips around in the area to admire nature and only brought one or two guards with her. On the very last day that they stayed there she was alone with Olaf away from the rest for awhile. He told her about the resentment that he felt for his own parents and the loyalty he felt for her.

"Oh thank you Olaf" she said and put her arm gently around him to comfort him. They were sitting like that for some time until they started to come even closer to each others, and suddenly the feelings of understanding and consolation had lost to a very strong feeling of lust that overpowered them and they committed adultery.

Thorhilde understood fully the gravity of what had happened and said to Olaf: "What happened should never have taken place. I have admonished the rest of us to stay clean, and I their Queen have broken my wows. We must keep proper distance in the future." Olaf looks unhappy too, but Thorhilde tells him squarely, "It was my fault. I am twice your age and should have known better. You are an innocent victim. Please forgive me!" They leave in silence and pretend that nothing has happened between them.

The Wampanoags told them that to the north of them are the hunting grounds of a confederation of tribes called The Abenaki Nation. They do not like trespassing on their territory so you better stay out at sea.

Before they depart, Thorhilde has a quiet talk with the Lord, and she asks for his forgiveness. She already knows she has conceived, and also knows that she is not going to take the baby away. The Native have ways of doing that by using herbs, but that easy way was not pleasing with the Lord, and she knew that she had offended him enough already.

The rest of the trip home went smoothly and they were home by mid July.

Guttorm met them and embraced them all and told them that things were going well for the settlers. Since Thorhildes expedition became delayed he had taken upon himself to allot the farm together with the settlers and the Shawnee chief. The settlers were all in a happy mood and had already started sowing planting and constructions of their homesteads. He also tells her that the expedition to the east coast had safely arrived home again, but they were still waiting for the western expedition to return.

Thorhilde was eager to hear the report from the returned eastern expedition, but Guttorm advised her to wait for all the settlers to be summoned, so that she could relay it to them all.

Since it would take until next day for the settlers to be coming, Thorhilde asked the crews from the two small ships that had been on the expedition to the Potomac River and the Deleware River systems to relay everything that had happened to them during their expedition, to her and the crew of the "Dragon of Greenland".

They met together in the church-come-assembly building and since both the two ships had partnered all the way the crews handpicked Einar to be their spokesman.

He starts saying "First I want to thank the Lord for that we are all safe and in good health and that we also have had this wonderful opportunity to learn and to enjoy such marvelous wonders that this land has to offer us. We have traveled through lands of imaginable beauty and have been helped and nourished by good fortune all the way. To follow the Ohio River was the most strenuous part of the journey. Luckily we had a Shawnee scout with us. Not long after we left, our Shawnee scout warned us that we had entered Erie hunting grounds and had to be ready for attacks. We stayed close together and slept on our swords and close to shields, bows and arrows. We came after some ten days of rowing to a large fork in the river and our Shawnee scout pointed to the southern loop of it. Soon we became encompassed by high mountains and had to often drag our small ship over shallower parts as well as drag them overland passed rapids and small falls.

Luckily for us it was berry season, and there was such a plentiful of wild delicious berries to be eaten that it is beyond imagination. There were plenty of deer to hunt for as well as fishes to be caught, and we enjoyed it as we never have before in our lives. We are all so thankful as to have been chosen to take part in it. Eventually we came to a large gap in the mountain ridge and manage to drag our ships across the ridge dividing the southern loop of the Ohio River and unto the Potomac River.

"Was not that very strenuous?" Thorhilde asked.

"Oh yes it was, but we were many to pull and push, and we are strong and healthy, so we eventually managed, but it took us several days to cross. There were snowcaps on the mountains in the distance. Our Shawnee scout had warned us to be completely silent going upstream the Ohio River and its tributaries so that we might be unseen by any Erie hunter that should so happen to be near by. He warned to speak very softly, since the sound of voices can carry far in a silent atmosphere, and a native hunter would be vey alert to anything that might cause his suspicion or curiosity. Also our scout warned us not to light any fires by night as long as we were on Erie hunting grounds. Luckily we managed to avoid being seen. Thanks to the Lord.

We then followed the Potomac River, and travelled through a most gorgeous landscape. It is almost impossible to even imagine the beauty of the Potomac River, the river banks and the Potomac River Valley. After a while we arrived at a native village on the northern bank of the Potomac River that our Shawnee scout said was an Algonquian speaking tribe belonging to the Piscataway Nation. "They will treat us friendly and I am also capable of communicating with them." Our scout told us, and so they did when we arrived.

They treated us to a delicious meal and were as friendly as could be."Be cautious in your further travels they warned us. To our north there is an Iroquoian speaking nation called Susquehannock Nation that is warlike and very unfriendly towards any trespassing on their hunting grounds. They are friendly to the five Iroquoian Nations further north and could become a dreadful potential enemy. Already they have started to trespass on our hunting grounds to try us out. They mainly have their hunting grounds around a large river called Susquahanna River that empties into the same large bay as the Potomac River, but further north." We followed their advice and stayed away from the hunting grounds of the Susquehannock Nation, but journeyed around the large bay peninsula by sea and upstream a large river that is the center of the of the hunting grounds of the Delaware Nation.

Our encounter with The Delaware Nation was a very pleasant one to us. They are blood brothers to the Shawnee Nation and they treated us accordingly, especially when they where told that Thorhilde had been made "High Queen of the Shawnee Nation". We were scouted upstream the Delaware River and all the surrounding area to the east of it. Returning back again, sailing north along the eastern coast of Vinland in good weather and we managed to sail and row upstream the Iroquoian River before the river started to freeze.

We have been here in the Ohio Settlement all winter and have been worried for you and the two smaller ships that still are on their western voyage. We know that the Lord has preserved you, and we are giving continuous thanks to him for that as well. Can we now all of us take part in a solemn prayer and fast for the well being of our brothers and sisters that are on the very dangerous and strenuous western expedition?"

The settlers now knew that they only had to hope and wait for news of their brothers and sisters that still were on, hopefully, their journey back home to the Ohio River settlement.

One day light fall, Thorhilde awakened by high pitched voices calling "Here they are coming; both the two ships are arriving!" All the settlers flocked towards the coming skips overjoyed with gladness to see them back again.

The crew of the ships came ashore tired and battered looking like soldiers coming back from a long war. They had stories of joy to tell and story of sadness. During the coastal passage they had lost several men and women after being attacked by some enormous bears on an island on the west coast.

Thorhilde and Guttorm consoled the crew and the parents of the deceased men and women as best as they could, but words can not bring young lives back again. The crew told them that they had buried the dead on an inner Aleutian island and had performed Christian burials for all of them.

They told the settlers that they had managed up to the Mandans without any problems. Since it had become so late in fall they accepted the invitation from the Mandan Nation to stay with them during the winter and only leave the next year when the continental division passes were free from snow.

With the help from Mandan and Shoshone scouts and of course with the help of Odin who was traveling with them, they found a natural way over the continental divide and from there down to Snake River and out into the ocean itself. It was a lot of work, but taking their time they managed without any problems. Entering the big western ocean was quite an experience for them. Now they were two small boats on a large ocean, and they knew that since it was already past midsummer and they had a long way to travel, they all decided to sail home as fast as they could in order to be there before ice would stop them.

Coming to a large and beautiful island in the Inner Aleutian Archipelago, they decided to rest for a few days. It was a most gorgeous island and there was an abundance of delicious berries to be picked and wild game as well. Not aware of any danger, a party of berry pickers left the camp in a very good mood and told the rest of the party that they would be back in a couple of hours. They were not in combat arms and the group consisted of five men and three women.

After some time the party at the camp heard some terrible shrieks for help, and at the same time they also heard horrible growls from something that must have been a large animal.

Harald that was the only survivor of the party told them: "We walked for some time to find a good place and had started picking berries when suddenly one of the women said "There is a cute little bear coming towards us, maybe he wants to taste some of our berries?" We were all watching in amazement at the scene and none of us really sensed the coming danger. Suddenly from nowhere came an enormous animal in such a fury that I cannot even to imagine to tell you. It leaped on the young woman and killed her straight out with one blow of his paw. Thereafter he turned on the rest of the party and as we had none combat weapons with us, there were no way that we could defend ourselves. With a horrendous speed it had killed or maimed seven of us and I only survived because I lied down and played dead. I could here my friends scream in horror of fear and death while the bear molded them to pieces and I only waited for my turn to come.

How I survived, I do not really know. Probably my time to die had not come yet, and the Lord held his hand over me. After some time the bear retreated together with his cub and as I rose up I could see that two from the party was still alive but bleeding heavily. I tried to render assistance but without any medical supply, I was helpless to stop them from bleeding to death.

The rest of the ship crew arrived in horror but were too late to be able to save any live but me. There were blood and body parts everywhere, and the rescuers broke down completely devastated. Some of them wanted to pursue the bear, but I begged them not to do so. The area was broken with plenty of steep hills in-between, given all the advantages to the mother bear. And what good would it had done to us if we could hunt it down and kill it with our combat weapons ready? Maybe more of us would die or even possible maimed and a baby bear left motherless by itself. We were trespassing on the bear's territory and the mother bear was only protecting her baby. I know that the rest of the crew disagreed with me in this matter, but we Vikings are entitled to our own opinions and I vied mine fearless of reprisals from the rest.

After the first shock of horror and the grief we all felt, we decided to return to our quarter. The dead bodies were carried along and we took a last farewell with them before they were buried. Our senior sailor conducted a solemn ceremony, and we all cried helplessly at their graves. From there we voyaged home as quickly as we could sail north of Vinland and over Lake Winnipeg back here."

All the listeners were touched by the story, and many took to their tears openly, even many men, and no one seemed to be ashamed by it.The next day Guttorm held a service of compassion for the dead and thanked the Lord for his grace and mercy that brought the survivors back safely.

Chapter XI

The Mandans and the Ohio River Settlement Massacre – 1332 – 33

Spring did arrive early in 1332 and Thorhilde had spent the winter wisely and had managed to organize the settlement to her liking. The farms were all of good sizes and were spread out over a large area, but for a small village at the center. The settlement had constructed a large church come cultural hall that also could serve as a school and if needed, a fortress for the settlers if needed.

The climate on this part of the Ohio River was temperate to mild in winter, and the settlers that were used to much harder climate, almost felt that they had arrived in Paradise.

Thorhilde remembered Gyda,s warning : "Be aware of good days, it might lead to idleness that again will lead to downfall. Comfortable societies will eventually loose respect for manual labor and try to find other people to do household chores for them a well as to till, plant, sow and harvest for them, eventually also to protect them and fight for them. Remember Sunshine" did she say: "The Lord expects us to do our part, before he steps in to protect us and helps us! Keep your people busy at all cost!"

She had started language classes in Siouan with Odin as the tutor, and the settlers had already started to become para proficient in it. They could not yet converse well in it, but did understand the meaning of the words and the expressions. Plans for the coming year were to bring the large ship up the Missouri River to the Mandan Nation and stay over the winter with them and return back again the coming spring. Already now she had come a long way in her thinking of how to shape a good future for the settlers in this land of promise.

Many times she wandered of what had happened to the three families that left the settlement. She knew Bjarni and his family well from The Northwestern Settlement of Greenland. They were all hard working and to a degree went on well enough with their neighbors, maybe mostly do to the fact that their farm was so isolated from the next, that chances for boundary conflicts were small. They were all very headstrong people as well as very physically strong. No one wanted them as enemies. And now they had become her enemies. She wandered if they were still alive, and if they were, what they were up to. Probably nothing good or to her liking, she thought to her as she wandered around the peaceful settlement in a quiet surrounding.

Guttorm had since he had broken with the arcdiose of Nidaros in distant Norway, also broken his wow of staying unmarried. He had married the second cousin of Thorhilde, a woman some twenty years younger than him and some ten years older than Thorhilde. Her name was Ingegjerd, and she was a highly respected woman both for her wisdom and for her integrity.

Thorhilde knew that she had to confess to him, and also wanted his wife to be present. They both welcomed her warmly and asked what they could do for her. Thorhilde starts by telling them both, everything what had happened, and can see that they are both stunned and shocked.

Ingegjerd is particular mean to her and says, "You are thirty six years old and have knowingly seduced and innocent boy at the age of eighteen How is this really possible? It is below anything thinkable. You are worse than a common whore. I am ashamed of being related to you." And she spits at her.

"Enough woman!", Guttorm shout at his wife. "Now you either behave with dignity, or leave us alone!"

Ingegjerd calms down, goes over to Thorhilde, and puts her arms around her and ask for her forgiveness.

Guttorm then counsel with the two women to try and mend what can be mended. They finally agree on that Thorhilde will go to the Mandans and Blackfoot as planned and have the mother of Singing Grass take care of the baby after she has born him in secrecy during the winter. "I can come with you as well and help you during your pregnancy", Ingegjerd states with vigor. I want your good name protected. "Take Olaf with you as well. He can be close to his own child and protect it if necessary."

"But what will the Lord think of me? Thorhilde is crying softly.

Guttorm puts his arms around her and says" Reciting the bible: Woman thy sins are forgiven. Go away and seen no more!"

Thorhilde leaves Guttorm and Ingegjerd with a light heart and knows that the Lord have forgiven her through his instruments, Guttorm and his wife.

Time came quickly for the departure of the "Dragon of Greenland" and its chosen crew. This time she was bringing with her Odin and Singing Grass as well as she had done changes to her crew in such a way that only unmarried men and women would travel together. Many of her former crew had found eternal partners and had been allotted farms of their own that needed to be attended to.

They all left in a happy mood, and as the last time she left Guttorm in charge of the Ohio settlement. As they journeyed up the Missouri River, Thorhilde admired the beauty of the rolling prairie on both banks. What a beauty and what a place to settle for a righteous people. Then she started thinking: "Are my people a righteous people?", and she was not too sure if they were. There was too much jealousy among them to class them as a righteous people. They were extreme independent, strong willed and hard people but the conflicts that sometimes did arise among them often had the core in hurt feelings. Feelings of inadequacy, unfairness and hurt pride often became unsolvable for them and they unfortunately looked for the solution in violence.

Probably that was the problem that Bjarni also had struggled with, and not being able to solve by himself. Even though she knew that he deserved what he got, she felt sorry for him and for his family." What will become of them in the after life?" She wondered for herself.

"Will we meet and reconcile in the next life?"

A lot of pushing and pulling of the large ship took its toll on them, but eventually they all reached the Mandan village safe and sound and Thorhilde knew immediately that she was among friends when she arrived. It was almost like seeing close family. Some of them were so light skinned that they looked far more like the Greenland Vikings than Native Vinlanders.

The elders and chiefs of the Mandans urged the Greenland Vikings to come and settle with them if the Ohio settlement should not work out. They told Thorhilde that they originated from the Ohio valley themselves.

Some three hundred years ago traders from Greenland came to their Ohio settlement and formed close connections to them that continued over a very long time. Many of the young men from Greenland had taken Mandan wives and made their homes with their tribe.

During the lap of time the Ohio settlement came into more and more conflicts with the Iroquois speaking tribes to their east and north, and they started a slow westward migration. They tried to settle on the prairie, and came into a very bloody conflict with the Pawnee nation, which almost half their numbers. Now we are safe here for the meantime, our only dangerous neighbors are the Lakota or Teton Sioux Nation to the north and to the west of us. The Shoshones further west does not bother us much, unless that they sometimes are on thieving raids in our area. They live on the continental divide and are masters in a quick disappearance.

They pleaded with Thorhilde and the Greenland Vikings to come and become one with them. She now understood well that if so was to happen they would loose their Nordic identity and also slowly their Nordic values and become more and more absorbed in the Mandan ways. The very thought of it frightened her. "What would Gyda advised her to do?"

Her mind became confused and she struggled with herself before she finally found concealment in talking with the Lord in a solemn prayer. "Please. Please my Lord, help me to make a correct decision in regard to our future here in this choice land of promise. I do not want my people to loose their Nordic roots and to forget their Christian upbringing." And she started crying "I want all the best for my people, but cannot do it alone. Please help me."

The Greenland Vikings stayed with the Mandans and enjoyed their hospitality for most of the summer.

Thorhilde asked the Mandan Chief if could provide scouts for her and a party to travel overland to the Blackfoot Nation. She wanted to bring with her Odin, Singing Grass and her personal guards as well. The Chief warned her that the Blackfoot's was a warlike tribe that did not like anybody trespassing on their territory, but Thorhilde felt confident that with the help of Odin that mastered their language and her own guard she would be able to persevere.

Before you leave, please party with us, the chief said to her. He seemed like he thought it was a farewell party for ever he wanted to throw for her and her guard.

They got themselves away early August and ventured through Assiniboine and Lakota Sioux hunting grounds for weeks before they arrived at the Blackfoot homeland.

One early morning they were surrounded by some dozen armed Blackfoot warriors, not too happy looking. Odin who spoke their language explained to them that they were seeking the mother of the little girl that was with them. The warriors didn't seem too happy with that explanation and came closer and mounted their weapons towards them. Thorhilde had instructed her guards to mount a tortoise shield around them if they became physically threatened and they managed to arrange a defensive formation so quickly as to discourage the Blackfoot warriors to attack them.

Again Odin tried to reason with them to let them pass on to their village and let the little Blackfoot girl meet with her mother. Out of nowhere the Blackfoot warriors suddenly attacked Odind and killed him. Thorhilde had her archers shower them with arrows and took down six of them.

They immediately retracted and left their dead and wounded behind.

Thorhilde had her men give Odin an Assiniboine burial, and they all mourned him for the faithful and good man he had been, and for all the assistance that he had rendered them and for all the invaluable information and knowledge that he had given.

Now Thorhilde and her men were determined to see the Blackfoot chief himself. She spoken broken Siouan and was capable of making herself understood by using gestures as well. With her she had her own personal guard of six highly trained warriors as well as forty young unmarried men and women, all of them highly skilled in combat. They did not fear the Blackfoot warriors.

Late at night they arrived at their camp and saw a lot of wigwams in front of them. The Viking warriors made a stand close to their camp and rested in defense position, ready for anything. In that position they stayed during the night and as morning arrived they proceeded in battle formation towards the largest tepee.

Coming close they were met by some elderly men that Thorhilde understood were the chiefs of the Blackfoot Nation. She also saw that they were treating the Vikings with an awe of respect du to the reputation that they already had yearned in the battlefield.

Thorhilde moved slowly, and with her personal guards close to her, towards the chiefs and motioned to Singing Grass that they wanted to see her mother.

The Blackfoot Chief smiled sarcastically and beckoned to one of his aids to get her. The Vikings got a shock when they saw her mother coming. She was small and battered looking, and had and extremely unhappy face. She was walking with a heavy limp.

"Can she come with us?" Thorhilde asked the Blackfoot Chief, pleadingly.

He answered with a sneer "Get her out of my sight before I kill her too!"

Thorhilde had her guard cover for her immediately, and order an organized retreat immediately. The party now returned in defense formation and made their way back to the Mandan village, always on their guard for a sudden attack. It seemed though that the Blackfoot Nation were well aware of their defense capacity and stayed away from a confrontation with them.

Well back and rested Thorhilde asked both Singing Grass and her mother Whispering Grass to come and stay with her while they were being entertained by the Mandan Nation. She did communicate understandably with Whispering Grass, and questioned her of why she had to give Singing Grass away to strangers.

"I had to do it in order for both of us to survive" Whispering Grass stuttered out her answer as if she was deeply shameful. "The Blackfoot Nation consists of very hard and merciless people."

"Please tell me what happened to both of you?" Thorhilde asked with tears in her eyes.

"When I gave birth to my little daughter that you are calling Singing Grass, I and my family soon discovered that she was different from other newborn children." Whispering Grass uttered it with melancholy in her voice.

"How did your family and tribe react and how did they treat you?" Thorhilde questioned her mildly.

"I know from my daughter that you are called Bleeding Heart because you are a mild and loving woman. The Blackfoot Nation consists of very hard and warlike people. They gave me neither mercy, nor help nor understanding, but left me to tend to her the best that I could. My husband even gave me a good beating when I refused to put her out in the forest to be devoured by wild animals. My daughter that you have taken in as your own daughter has also told me that you are willing to accept me as your blood sister and let us be sisters for eternity. Is this true Bleeding Heart?"

Thorhilde could not keep her tears back from streaming down her cheeks and embraced the little battered and beaten Blackfoot woman and held her closely unto her. "That is the truth Whispering Grass, where I go, you shall go with me!"

"Bleeding Heart, we are now blood sisters and I will go where you go, and your God will be my God."

Time went slowly by and during winter months, Ingegjerd is always close to Thorhilde and assists her in all possible ways. Thorhilde stays inside a lot and manage well to hide her pregnancy from the rest of the settlement, Vikings as well as Mandans. One very cold night in the middle of the winter Thorhilde gives birth to a little healthy looking boy and they name him Eric after Eric the Red.

To shield Thorhilde from shame, Ingegjerd pretend that she is the mother of the child, and they are all happy for her. Ingegjerd asks The Blackfoot woman "Whispering Wind" to be the nanny for the child and also even without Thorhilde knowing it, asks Olaf to marry Whispering Wind and be the guardian of the child.

It stuns Thorhilde when she is told, and she asks Ingegjerd "What did he say?"

"He accepted that immediately", she answered.

The marriage between the two was performed in beauty both in Viking, Blackfoot and Mandan custom. Thorhilde now felt at ease and thanked the Lord, Guttorm and Ingegjerd for all their assistance.

They stayed with the Mandan Nation for the winter and come spring the next year they made themselves ready to leave for the return to the Ohio River settlement as soon as the Missouri River allowed them to journey on it.

An early beautiful June morning they were approaching the settlement, and as they came closer they sensed immediately that something was far wrong. Coming even closer, they didn't see any animals grazing as usual, and the whole atmosphere was like a warning about the happening of a catastrophic event.

When landing their ships they were met by some hysteric elderly women that were shouting in agony "The Erie Nation has attacked us and have killed half of us! May the Lord be with us! Why did you leave us here without the warriors to protect us?"

Thorhilde knew instantly that they had protection enough if they had only been alert, but did not argue with the women. She sensed their grief and horror and asked to see Guttorm.

"He is dead!" one of the women answered. "Ragnhilde killed him herself and have written a message in blood for you to see on the Church wall." They took her to the building itself and before they entered they showed her the writing "This is for Bjarni, and you Thorhilde is the next one to suffer my revenge!"

It gave Thorhilde the shivers, not with fear but she sensed the hatred that Ragnhilde had harbored against her and the settlers. "How can anybody commit atrocities like that against former friends and neighbors?" She thought for herself. As they entered the large church building, they were met by armed men that were guarding the doorways. Inside were huddled together the survivors with what they had left of belongings.

Baard, the assistant priest was wounded but alive and he came and gave Thorhilde a resume of what had happened. "It all started only a couple of days ago. One early morning when just the daylight was starting to peek through the trees and bushes that there are so many of in this so otherwise tranquil and wonderful settlement, hundreds upon hundreds of Erie warriors surprise attacked us.

They must have been in hiding close to our farms for most of the night to have the full advantage of the surprise. Their faces and torsos were all painted in war colors and they were a frightful sight as they came screaming in anger towards us. What did surprise me and the other settlers was not that the Erie's would come against us, but that all adult members of the three families that left us were with them. All of them, including the women had shaved their heads like the Erie's have, and the men had painted their naked torsos in war colors as well.

They must have joined the Erie Nation and become blood brothers with them.

The worse one of them was Ragnhilde, the widow of Bjarni. You would not have believed her rage and hatred towards us all unless you actually had witnessed it as I and many others of us did. They first attacked the most outlying farms in our settlement quietly, and had it not been for that one young boy of twelve years old had managed to flee and to raise the alarm, they might have killed all of us."

Thorhilde was listening in stunned silence and blaming herself for not having taken precautions enough. Baard sensed it and calmed her by saying "It wouldn't have made things much better if you had been here. Then you and your warriors might have become surprised attacked and killed as well. Now at least we have you here to help us to survive"

"Please tell me what happened further, Baard?" Thorhilde asked him.

"I live close to the large combined church come community hall and fortress and was alarmed so early that I managed to organize our defense. First I ordered the alarm to be sounded and to call all settlers to come towards the church hall and to seek refuge inside that secure building. Having done that, I sent one very quick footed messenger to the Shawnee Chief asking for his immediate assistance.

Thirdly I had all the young boys and girls between six and twelve years old including to older experienced archers to loosen all of our ships, and tie them together and row them out in the middle of the river and steer them downriver to the first southern tributary river to the Ohio River, and there to secure them upstream and wait for help from either us, the Shawnee or from your party that we knew were on your way.

Most of the settlers managed to come here alive but did not manage to secure their animals before they came. They all had stories of horror to tell. The Erie warriors were not the worst ones, but the Greenland Vikings that were now their blood brothers and sisters. The women were as bad as the men, if not worse. Ragnhilde seemed to have been in command of the party. She was all covered in human and animal blood and she screamed like a demon from Hell itself.

When we were all inside the church hall and also had mounted archers on the towers, we eventually started to feel somewhat safe. The Erie war party then by command of Ragnhilde, then ordered the church surrounded and put to the torch. They were eagerly putting up stocks of firework around it to make it burn, even though we had archers in the towers to shoot at them, Ragnhilde had made them protective shields, and for a while it seemed like that we would have to leave the building and to face them openly outside. There were so many of the attackers that it seemed to me that they were exceeding a thousand or being close to that number.

Then suddenly to our great relief, our blood brothers the Shawnee Nation came to our assistance, and it surprised the Erie's so much, that they became disorganized for a while. We then decided to let most of our armed men and women leave the fortress and join in with the Shawnee warriors.

Ragnhilde left screaming and cursing. But she did not leave before that she had Guttorm beheaded in front of us, and written the message on the church that you already have read. They had him tied and ready to be killed. She screamed to us "Your God could not protect your priest. Now the time is coming for your so-called Queen. Let us now see if your God will protect her, you weaklings!"

Together with the Shawnee Nation we managed to take an inventory of the damage. All of our outlying farms are completely destroyed. They have even viciously slaughtered all the animals, even cats and dogs, and have torched the houses. As well they have killed both Sevat and Haakon with their Cree and Assiniboine princess wives, together with their newborn children. Their bodies they have mutilated as wild animals, and I find it hard to believe that any human being can sink that low.

We even heard her given the orders to the Erie warriors that they were to see to that all the horses were to be killed. Do not leave anything for them to be able to breed new ones. Also kill and destroy anything seen to be useful to them for the future. The hours that we suffered waiting inside the building while being surrounded by this murderous band of Erie warriors and their blood brothers, the evil Vikings could best be prepared to the waiting room for Hell. When we were sure that they all had left, we decided to stay close together and wait for you and your party to return. Thorhilde, I do not think that you can fully appreciate who glad we are to see you back here with us again."

"Can we all meet together today and discuss what we are to do immediately and what our future plans will be!" Thorhilde now saw the need for urgent actions and decision makings. Baard called them all together and said "Since Guttorm has become martyred, I am now you only priest and responsible for your spiritual welfare. Terrible things have happened to our settlement recently and we that are alive are thankful for the protection that an omnipotent and merciful Lord provided for us. Thorhilde, our elected queen has called us together for us to act upon the necessities of this day and also for us to plan our future."

Thorhilde faces the battered and stricken settlers and become so filled with emotions that she can hardly speak but starts to stutter. "I am so stricken with emotion that I find it hard to speak to you at this time. First I think that we need to take inventory of who of us that survived and who of us that is dead. Let us start and count the living settlers!" The whole process takes about an hour and when they are all done, there are with the crew from "The Dragon of Greenland" and the young boys and girls that are still guarding the ships further down river one thousand and forty four of us still alive.

"That means that seven hundred and eighty three of us have left this world and are now with their forefathers." Baard had been in charge of the numbering and recording.

"First of all we must give them all a Christian burial." Thorhilde said and we will plan our future.

The task of bringing all the dead bodies close to the church took the rest of the day. They were all laid out family-vise in front of the church so that friends and families could take a last farewell with them.

Thorhilde visited all the farms with her guard and was still in a numbed shock of what she had seen of bestiality and destruction. Many of the bodies were so mutilated and so burned that they were almost beyond recognition. But by knowing what farm that they belonged to they were for sure able to identify them.

Earlier she had sent "The Dragon of Greenland" down river to bring back the smaller ships and their young crew. "Prepare the young boys and girls for the worst," she admonished the men of the large ship, "so that they do not get the shock of their life when they see all the dead bodies."

It was getting late and they stayed close together.

Thorhilde questioned them if they wanted the dead people buried or if they should burn them together with the church. She says "This is not a safe place for us anymore. Let us as soon as we can, collect anything that is valuable and preserve able and leave for the Mandan Settlement on the Missouri River. They have already invited us to come and live with them. We shall avenge this with Ragnhilde and the Eries later this summer when we are ready and prepared for it. This time the advantage shall be ours. We shall surprise attack them. Who is in favor of that we burn the bodies together with the church building when we leave tomorrow night?"

"Is this the right way to do it? "One of the settlers asks in surprise.

"If we bury them the normal way, our enemies might return and shame their bodies or feed them to their pigs or even eat them like wild beasts. Ragnhilde is now capable of anything bad!" Thorhilde almost didn't believe her own words as she spoke them.

That seemed to settle the discussion.

Thorhilde sent for the Shawnee Chief and she wanted to explain to him why she wanted to leave so early, and to request a scout from him that knew where the Erie's had their quarters.

All the dead bodies were carried inside the large communal church building and lied out in a respectful manner ready for the next day service. They were all on full alert for a second surprise attack and had their ships heavily guarded as well.

"Under no circumstance shall they be able to destroy our ships." she spoke to herself. "I shall defend them to my death myself."

The night went without any further incidents and the next morning as they awoke, the Shawnee Chief and a group of Shawnee warriors had arrived. He told Thorhilde that for the Erie's to commit such atrocities, they had to be led by someone else. They are not that bad people, he said.

Thorhilde told him that due to his help, the settlers had been saved, and that she was to avenge the massacre later on. "I hope that we haven't put your nation at risk?" she asked him.

"Not at all!" The Shawnee Chief answered. We wish you all the best of luck on your further journey through your life. May the great and Merciful Spirit that rules everything be with you our blood brothers.

The settlers filled the church with firewood to make the destruction of the human flesh total. Nothing was to be left for any returning Erie or their blood brooder Vikings to shame or mistreat. Baard first conducted a sermon of passion where he read all the names of the deceased and all of their families were given the last chance to take farewell with their families, friends and loved ones before the building were put to the torch.

Soon they were all onboard the little fleet of ships and they anchored them midstream to watch the church burn and their dead ones go to their ancestors.

Chapter XII

Her final journey and revenge on the Erie Nation – 1333

One day in early July, they all arrived safely at the Mandan Village and were received with a fantastic hospitality and compassion. It warmed the hearts of hardened Greenlanders to see the emotion that these very friendly people had for them. These people are our true brothers in Christ, Baard told Thorhilde. "Do you think that we may convert them to Christianity?"

"Never give up hope Baard!" Thorhilde answered him. "However there is one thing that puzzles me and that is the Christian Doctrine of Forgiveness. We are asked to always forgive our enemies and to let the Lord take his vengeance in his own due time. Are we supposed to forgive Ragnhilde for her actions? Was it from the very beginning my fault when I corrected Bjarni to discharge his oxen from and overloaded ship? Should I better have let them take that chance themselves?"

"No Thorhilde, it was not your fault that you ordered him to discharge of some cargo to give the ship more freeboard. He has always been a stubborn troubler and had to face the consequence of his own actions. When it comes to forgiveness, we are commanded to do so, but we are also to serve justice. And when it comes to Ragnhilde and her Viking followers, justice should here be served with death sentences. The problem is really what to do with their smaller children. They are innocent in the actions of their parents, but I have discussed this with all of the household elders, and they agree with me that they will grow up with a horrible hatred towards us and will probably dedicate their lives to destroying us and the Mandan Nation."

"How can they possibly do that, they live so far away from us?" Thorhilde was surprised.

"Hatred knows no boundaries. They will find ways to afflict us. I have contemplated it and studied the scriptures and prayed to the Lord for answers and feel that the answer is found in the Old Testament where the Israeli tribes are commanded to utterly destroy all the inhabitants of the land to avoid them to become a problem to them later.If the Lord saw fit to command Israel to do that, why should not we protect our people for the future as well? Had we destroyed the three families that left us altogether then, instead of allowing them to leave, things maybe would have worked out for us in our beautiful Ohio River Settlement!"

Thorhilde is stunned and in shock by his reasoning. "Are you sure Baard that this is what the Lord wants us to do?"

"My Queen, you are the sovereign over us and have to give the command, but I have a feeling that the settlers will kill them all regardless of what you command them to. They are that upset and vengeful."

"Thank you Baard for your advice, will I be held accountable to the Lord for the killing of small children?" Thorhilde was almost crying.

"You are now first of all, in this trial time of ours, accountable for how you are securing the future of your people." Baard is consistent in his arguing.

"I take your point Baard, but this is so serious that I want the Nordic Thing to be convened. The Thing has the highest authority among us, and I will have to bow down to their decisions. Let us meet as soon as possible."

The Thing is convened, and all the Nordic settlers above the appropriate age of both genders was already assembled when Thorhilde came to the Thing dressed in her Royal Regalia. She felt that she should do so out of respect to Viking Law in particular and for the settlers and the far off but watching Mandan Nation in general. Baard started by reciting the old Viking Law for them, and he particularly dwelt with the authority that was granted to the sovereign King or Queen and the authority that was granted to the Thing itself. It was like that he was expecting differences between Thorhilde and the Thing.

Thorhilde asked to be allowed to address the Thing "I am your elected Queen and you have all sworn loyalty to me. This is of course due to the fact that I as your Commander in Chief must have executive power in order for me to act quickly if needed. I am very well aware of the fact that the authority of the Thing, is above my executive authority. Even above the authority of the Thing is the Viking Law that Baard just recited for us all. But one more Law is above the Viking Law, and that is the commandments of the Lord.

I will subdue to any decision by the Thing that do not violate the Viking Law or The Commandments of the Lord. Baard and I have had a very deep discussion of what we ought to do, and have come to an agreement that I will now put before the Thing for a vote after all of you that want to comment on my proposal have done so. The acts of horror that Ragnhilde and the three families did commit against us, were so horrible that it is beyond human recognition. My proposal to the Thing is that we organize a punitive expedition against them this fall, and put all members from these three families to death. If we do not root out this evil from this land now, it will become an everlasting scourge for our descendants. Both Baard and I myself have studied the scriptures and have also inquired of the Lord if we also should put down even the smaller children. We got the answer that; we had no other options but to protect our settlers and our descendants. When it comes to the Erie Nation, it will be different. Here we will only take the lives of any armed Erie warrior that will be a threat to us. This is my proposal to the Thing!"

There was a lot of chatter and quite some murmuring among the settlers.

One of them spoke "Why should we spare the Erie Nation after all that they did to us? Time now, is not for niceties!" He was highly applauded and Thorhilde knew that she had to be cautious with her reasoning to the Thing.

"Our Shawnee blood brothers informed me that what the Erie Nation became a part of, was not their way of settling differences. They had to be tricked or fooled into the attack by a devious mind. If wee completely root out the three Nordic Viking families, the evil among them will be gone with them."

"I think that we shall exterminate the whole Erie Nation" One of the surviving widows proposed and was vividly applauded.

Thorhilde sensed the feeling of revenge and hatred from the settlers and for a while it numbed her. "Do not let us become as bad as Ragnhilde and the three families. We are Christians and must also obey the commandment that says: "Though shall not shed innocent blood". If we kill defenseless women and unarmed children, we might find ourselves in Hell together with Ragnhilde in the next life. I refuse to lead you against any defenseless women and children. Make your choice here and now!"

Baard addressed the Thing and supported her as well as did also many of the survivors. The vote of the Thing came to accept Thorhildes proposal, but it was not done with ease.

Thorhilde again addressed the Thing and put forward another proposal "I want to be the foremost in the attack, and I feel that this might be my last journey. I ask for you to sustain me in my strategy, and if I should die during the battle, I want to be buried onboard "The Dragon of Greenland" and that with me the Royal Regency of The Free Northwestern Settlement of Greenland shall end. This land shall be free from the aristocracy of the old world."

The Thing went silent. All chattering and murmuring had stopped, and it was like a solemn peace took control of the Thing, and they all left quietly and in peace.

Thorhilde went to her bed both physically and mentally exhausted, hoping that a rest would clear her mind for the important decisions that would be needed to be taken in the near future. Next day she spent together with the two Blackfoot women. She relayed all her hopes and sorrows on to them and felt that they both knew in their hart that they this time was to part from each others fore ever in this life.

Whispering Grass said to her "Bleeding Heart, I know that you soon are to meet with the Great Spirit. You will also meet with your husband, children, mother and father as well as your grandmother. It will become a joyous meeting for you. Will you come and welcome me and Singing Grass when we die and have met the Great Spirit?"

"Of course I will my beloved friends; I am already looking forward to it."

Singing Grass said to Thorhilde "Among the Blackfoot we have a tradition that when we know that somebody is to die, we sing and hymn for them. Do you want us to do that for you Bleeding Heart?"

"Oh please do that for me." Thorhilde answered with gladness.

The three women seated themselves in a circle and Singing Grass started to hymn in a melodically voice the old Blackfoot death song.

Considering the gravity of the situation, Thorhilde only felt peace and calm, and after a while started to follow the hymning of the Blackfoot women. How long they were like that she didn't know, but when she awoke, she saw that the two women had placed her very carefully on her bed and covered her with blankets of deer hide. She awakened with a clear mind, and it was like all problems that she felt was mounting on her, was gone.

Whispering Grass was waiting smilingly together with the more serious looking Singing Grass. We have prepared food for you Bleeding Heart, come and eat with us. The Great Spirit did allow you to peak into his kingdom while you were sleeping. Could you feel his presence Bleeding Heart?"

"I did fell an immense peace. Was that the Great Spirit?" Thorhilde asked.

"Yes it was, and this is the first thing that you will feel before you meet him and your family after you death Bleeding Heart."

Thorhilde met with the warriors to discuss the strategies of the attack. They all agreed upon a night attack during a full or almost full moon to have the advantage of the surprise, and to catch them off guard. "We must first of all know where Ragnhilde and the three families are lodging so that we can head straight for them immediately. Why don't we send our Shawnee scout out beforehand to scout out for us where they are?"

"The Erie's will have guards at their canoes and also at their villages. We must silence them beforehand so that they cannot raise the alarm. Ragnhilde and the three families are that cowardice that they will try to hide behind the Erie warriors if they have a chance for it. We must get to know where the three families are beforehand, other wise we will not succeed in destroying them all." One of the more experienced warriors warns them.

Thorhilde says "We will travel with all our ships and seven hundred armed men and women. Left will be children younger than twelve years old and a guard of fifty warriors. There will be a total mobilization of our forces. Coming to our destination, we will leave our ships some safe distance from the shore, and with the oldest one hundred and fifty men and women to guard them. This will leave us five hundred and fifty highly skilled and dedicated warriors for the attack.The more we are capable of surprising them, the better. We will do our outmost to come unseen even if it means sailing and rowing by night on the northern side of Lake Erie, until we have to cross over to the south banks of the lake.

Erie's are infamous for using poisonous arrows. We must cover our bodies with deer hide thick enough to withstand penetration. Also everyone in the advance unit must carry shields, and if possible helmets."

Before their departure Thorhilde did not sleep much. She thought of all the tremendous possibilities that the Ohio River Settlement could have had, if it had been left in peace. The settlement could have increased rapidly in numbers, and since there was open access to the oceans of the worlds over the Ohio and the Mississippi Rivers, they could have constructed large keel ships and sailed the oceans, even to Europe. There they could have absorbed new inventions into their culture and traded where they wanted to.

Even new settlers from Iceland and perhaps also from Norway could have been encouraged to come over and settle "A New Norway "and become shielded from the exploitation of the King of Norway.

She cried herself into sleep one night and thought to herself "My Lord, my Lord, Why-Why-Why did you not stop Ragnhilde in her devious plan?"

The next morning she was all alert again and the last preparing for the journey was made. Since they were to attack close to the last full moon in August and needed about three weeks for their journey, and Thorhilde saw to that everything was going according to plan.

Sailing down the Missourie River could be quite a challenge, especially with the large warship "The Dragon of Greenland". Often they had to take the ships overland passed rapids, but they were many and experienced, and it was down hill.

Thorhilde even had time to again admire the beauty of the rolling prairie on both sides of the river as they came close to the Mississippi River. The party rowed their ships up the Mississippi and Illinois rivers until they again had to drag them overland to the southern loop of the Chicago River. From the Chicago River they sailed north on Lake Michigan and south on Lake Huron until they one day in late August were on Lake Erie itself.

Their Shawnee scout advices them to maneuver their ships close to one of the desolate islands close to the place where they were to disembark their warriors. By early morning one day in late August they are close enough to see their landing place, but still have their ships in good hiding. When night comes the Shawnee scout paddle ashore in a native bark-canoe that they have brought with them for that purpose. He told them that he knew where the Erie's had their villages, but was not sure of which one of them would house the three Viking families.

Thorhilde asked him to also locate their guards and search for the safest route to the village.

They waited in awe for the coming back of their Shawnee scout and to their surprise they saw that he was returning with a native Erie warrior. He sensed their fear but beckoned to them that he was a friend, and that they had nothing to fear from him. The Erie native was a fearful looking man in his mid thirties, but without war paint, he was almost handsome looking. Their Shawnee scout told them that he had caught him off guard and had taken him prisoner.

"He has given me his word with an oath that he will not escape, but stay with us." Their Shawnee scout told them.

"Can we trust him?" Thorhilde asked.

"If an Erie Native gives his word in an oath, he will keep it. It will have eternal consequences for him if he breaks it, and he does not want to be called "Se there is the Erie warrior that broke his word of oath, what shall we call him!" The shame will follow him through all his travels on the eternal hunting grounds. You can be completely sure that he will keep his word to us."

Thorhilde and her warriors now felt secure and were happy that they could now relay on first hand information of the Erie Nation and their settlements.

The Erie warrior told them that he was unmarried and asked for Thorhildes permission to join their war party and become one of their tribe. He seemed puzzled by the size of "The Dragon of Greenland" and openly admired their armor and Nordic features. He told them that he knew where the Vikings were lodging and that he would gladly lead them there. "They are very evil people he said and it will only be good for the Erie Nation to get rid of them.

Ragnhilde and the three families had come to them and asked for mercy and help to settle and to become their blood brothers. They had to pass through a very demanding initiating process including torture conducted by the Erie women as was their custom. They were all courageous and tough people and passed their initiating test to the admiration of the Erie women so well that a couple of unmarried young boys were chosen to be their husbands. The Erie's admire courage above everything and the Nordic Vikings had plenty of it. In a very short time their leader Ragnhilde became one of their leaders and started to plan the destruction of the Viking Ohio River Settlement that Thorhilde and her followers so eagerly had recently begun to settle."

"But how can an elderly woman like Ragnhilde maneuver herself into such a prominent position. I thought that the men are the leaders among the natives." Thorhilde asked the Erie warrior in surprise.

"Not among the Iroquois Nations. They are matriarchal. The lineages of their kings follow the female lineages, and the women have as much to say in any affair of the tribe as the men. Anciently we were also cannibals, but do only follow this old tradition if we feel a need for it." Their Erie friend answers.

"When will that be needed then?' Thorhilde asked.

"They make a stew of the brain of a wise man or the heart of a strong man to inherit wisdom and strength." The Erie warrior saw that they were shocked but consoled them. We will be victorious tomorrow morning but we must act in silence and also act fast. If the Erie nation gets alerted, warriors from all the villages will come to their assistance."

"How did Ragnhilde manage to have the Erie's attack us? We were not on their land!" Thorhilde asked.

"She told the Erie's at a mass meeting that the settlers at the Ohio River had plans to enlarge their settlements gradually further and further in time and that it was a wise decision to attack and destroy them completely before they became too many and too strong."

"Did the Erie's believe her?" Thorhilde asked again

"It seemed to make reason to the tribe and they agreed that she could have one thousand warriors with her and mount a surprise attack on the settlement. I was not a party to the attack."

"You will lead us tomorrow. Let us rest and wait for darkness." Thorhilde ordered.

Darkness came and provided the necessary coverage for their landing and the almost full moon gave them just sufficient light to see where to go. As Thorhilde had ordered, the ships with the elderly pulled away from the shore sufficient enough to be safe from a surprise attack but near enough to come to immediate assistance if needed.

Their Erie Warrior friend told them that the quickest way to the village where the three families were would take about one hour but that they would take a different route that was twice as long but much safer. "When we return back to Lake Erie, we will take the shortest and quickest route" He said. "Erie warriors will come after us from all their villages when they know of the attack and they may raise as many as four thousand warriors. Beware of them, they are a dangerous enemy. Do not torch any of the houses. That will only alarm all the Erie villages at once. Do what you have to do quickly and let us retreat immediately before they can organize a full scale attack on us. They will outnumber us six to one."

The war party proceeded quietly and stopped close to the village where the three families had their lodgings. A native guard could be seen on the top of a little hill nearby. Thorhilde ordered the Erie warrior and the Shawnee scout: "Silence him at all cost and report back here immediately there after!"

Luckily for them all, the guard was silenced and Thorhilde did not ask how that happened, but asked the Erie warrior Lead the Vikings to their houses, and me in particular to Ragnhilde;s house. I want to deal with her myself.

They split up and made themselves ready to attack every house in the large village simultaneously. Thorhilde handpicked the most experienced warriors to attack the lodgings of the three families. They were now according to the Erie warrior occupying some fourteen huts.

Daylight had just started to come through the trees and brush surrounding the village, and the timing was ideal for a total surprise. Now was the time for payback, Thorhilde thought with a cold smile on her face. No more niceties from us.

Thorhilde waited patiently until they all beckoned that they were all set for a surprise attack, and signaled a quiet sign of attack. With six of her personal guards along with her she entered a large room. They could see several people sleeping on hides on the floor and Thorhilde told her guards "Kill them all but leave Ragnhilde for me!"

Quite commotions started, and Thorhilde eventually saw which one of them was Ragnhilde. She was dressed like and looked like an Erie woman, just more evil looking. Her guards had starting the killings of everyone in the room but for Ragnhilde and when she realized that she was the next to die, she started to plead for mercy.

"Please do not kill me too Thorhilde. You are a good Christian woman and cannot do this to me. I am truly sorry for what happened, but we had no choice but to follow the Erie Nation. They demanded it of us!"

"You liar!," Thorhilde said angrily and thrust her sword through her torso. Blood gushed from Ragnhilde;s open mouth and her chest wound and Thorhilde withdrew her sword and severed her head from her body before she calmed down and commanded her guard to leave the house and take inventory of the attack. Her warriors reported that they had killed everyone inside the houses that the three families were occupying. Altogether there were some one hundred and twenty huts in that particular village and the destruction to it was total. Her warriors had not left a single sole to live and raise the alarm.

Thorhilde now understood that for the safety of the war party it was important that no one could escape and raise the alarm. There were thousand of armed and ready warriors now awakening close to them and it was only a matter of time before they had the whole Erie Nation after them."Start an organized retreat immediately. Stay in defense formation and be as fast and quiet as possible." She ordered. They had traveled for about half an hour and could now clearly see Lake Erie and the awaiting ships, when they suddenly heard war cries behind them.

"Hurry, they are coming at us!" The Erie warrior shouted.

"Run as fast as you can!" Thorhilde shouted.

She knew that the Erie warriors were quicker on their feet than the Vikings and she did not want to be cut off from the ships. When half of the Viking war party had arrived on the southern bank of Lake Erie, and were ready to go onboard the ships, hundreds of screaming Erie warriors was coming so close as to shower them with arrows. Thorhilde knew that their war arrows were poisonous and hoped that they had been in such a hurry that they were only shooting at them with normal hunting arrows without poison.

"Let me and one hundred Viking warriors stop and secure the rear retreat!" she shouted. "The rest of you enter the ships and mount your archers to defend our retreat." While retreating slowly, she suddenly felt like a sting from a wasp in her right hand and immediately knew that she had been hit by a poisonous arrow. Obviously the Erie warriors were aiming at her. They saw her outfit and knew instantly that she was the Viking Queen.

"Make a quick and organized retreat towards the ships!" She ordered. "The ships crews will protect us while we board the ships." They could all now clearly see that Thorhilde was the prime prey for them. Some of their warriors even entered the water and wielded their tomahawks in anger because they were just seconds too late to reach her.

"See to that we are all onboard before we depart!" she shouted.

The scene on the bank was unbelievable. As the ships were rowed slowly away from the banks, hundreds upon hundreds of Erie warriors were lying dead or maimed on the ground, while many of them came swimming towards the ships with tomahawks ready.

Thorhilde could not but admire their fighting spirit. They would have been good to have as friends but could also be dreadful enemies. She also knew that they could lay in wait for them in the narrow sound and river that separated Lake Erie from Lake Huron. On part of that journey they would even have to drag their ships ashore passed rapids as well.

She made a quick decision.

"We are to form a V formation with the two smaller ships up front and "The Dragon of Greenland" at the center of the fleet.

Let us proceed as quickly as possible by sail and oars to Lake Huron before the Erie Nation possible can organize an attack on us when we are vulnerable. They can not probably come that quickly overland or even by canoes. They won't be able to come before us over such a long stretch of water." She had not even said it before they saw that the Erie nation was coming at them in their war canoes.

The warriors in their painted war canoes came closer and closer and there were virtually hundreds of them making it a fearful scenario. But now the Vikings had the upper hands, being onboard larger ships with experienced archers ready to defend them. As wave upon wave of them came close enough for their archers to strike them they eventually had to give up, and with shrieks of anger turn away. Even though the Vikings knew that they were out of immediate danger, they knew well of the narrow pass that they had to pass through before entering into the larger Lake Huron.

They rowed their ships up into full speed until they caught the wind and sailed at a good speed westward on Lake Erie. Early next day they were at the narrows between Lake Erie and Lake Huron and could see that they were being watched from ashore. To their luck, they had arrived so early as not to give the Erie Nation time enough to mount a larger war party in place to stop them. Even the part of the journey where they had to drag their ships overland went without any problems.

They heard animal and bird signals that their Erie warrior friend told them were Erie war signals. "However they are too far away from us to harm us he said further. We are also to come close to the shores when we are leaving Lake Huron and are entering into Lake Michigan he continued, but they are on the hunting ground of a different tribe and the area is not that dangerous to us."

Two of the crew but for Thorhilde had also been hit by poisonous arrows and were in not a too good shape. One of the younger unmarried women that was with Thorhilde on "The Dragon of Greenland" had been hit in her neck and was almost for sure going to suffer death. She was in a terrible agony and took her pain with a calm smile on her face.

She holds Thorhildes hand hard and says to her "My beloved Queen, I am so happy that I have been able to have sailed with you on many of your trips and consider it a great honor of having been your friend. I hope that our friendship will last forever and that we shall meet in the other world. Farewell Bleeding heart." And she closed her eyes and died.

They mourned her and held a Christian burial ceremony for her before they dressed her and swept her in deerskin. They left her sword with her in order to sink her to the bottom of the lake and entered her body into the sea.

The second victim was a young man that had a hit in his arm. He had immediately made a deep cut in the wound and had spit out the poison and looked to be a survivor. He was though weak and pale looking but Thorhilde and the rest of the crew was cheering him up, and they all felt that he due to his young age and good physic together with the quick action that he had taken when he became hit, would heal him completely. But he needed to rest.

Thorhilde herself had suppressed her own war wound as if nothing had happened but now as they were approaching the narrows where Lake Huron and Lake Michigan meets, it became obvious to everyone that she too was a victim of the poisonous arrows. She almost fainted while standing upright and the crew came to see what was wrong.

"You have been hit too our Queen, why didn't you request our help?" one woman asked.

"I had other things to see to, and the poison is taking its told on me. This is to be my last journey."

"Let us take off some of your clothes so that we can dress the wound!" the woman insisted.

"Give me my privacy; don't undress me in front of the whole crew!" Thorhilde said angrily.

"We will make a shield around you. But let us take a look at your arm" The women that were now surrounding her were in shock when they saw that most of her right arm had become both blue and green and yellow and had also started to stink. The oldest of them said to Thorhilde "There is only one way that we can save your life my Queen, and that is to immediately amputate your right arm just below your shoulder."

Thorhilde frowned at the request and said "No one of you is to touch my body anymore. I forbid it."

She could hear them discussing softly with the men what to do, and one of the women told her that the crew had made the decision that they would amputate whatsoever she said in order to save her life.

The Viking Queen shouted to her guard. "Do not let any body touch my body. Use your weapons to defend me if necessary. "Her guard formed a circle around her and mounted their swords in order to stop any one from coming towards her.

The older and most experienced of the women said to her guards. "Are you aware of that you are sentencing her to death?"

"We have our orders and will obey her." The captain of her guard answered. It is her decision not to have her body mutilated. Give her that respect and refrain from trying to impose what you think is good for her down her as well as all the rest of us."

"Now we are having a dying queen to care for. Do you mind if we comfort her?" One of the women asked sarcastically.

"Not at all!, but do not disobey her in her last will. If she want do die here onboard "The dragon of Greenland" on this very journey, let her have it her way." The captain of the guard answered her.

As they sailed south on Lake Michigan, Thorhilde became gradually worse and started to hallucinate. She felt that she was in a large and beautiful field with all the spring and summer flowers that she remembered from her childhood in Greenland. It was like she was seated among the flowers and some of her childhood friends were also there.

It was such a beautiful place that she felt it difficult to leave it.

She awakened when they had to pull the ships from the southern loop of the Chicago River and unto the Illinois River. When they were on sufficient water again on the Illinois River she was clear enough to call all the household elders onboard "The Dragon of Greenland" for her last instructions.

"When we soon now will enter the Mississippi River, I am ready to depart this life and to enter into the next life. I have honestly tried my best to lead you and guide you, but have not always succeeded as you saw happened with Bjarni and his family. After me there shall be none Kings nor Queens to guide you, but follow the commandments of the Lord.

I request that you burn me onboard "The Dragon of Greenland" on the Mother of all rivers, the Mighty Mississippi River where she meets with the beautiful Ohio River.

Please see to that our Shawnee scout are brought safely back to his own people and thank the Shawnee Chief for everything that he has done for us all. Without his help, we might all have been dead. Now I want to sleep! Farewell for now."

The fleet was approaching the Mississippi and Thorhilde was now so weak that they knew that she wouldn't last long. There was a very sadden mood hanging over them all. They had all loved her and respected her for her courage, diligence and leadership abilities. Most of all they loved her for her compassion towards anyone that were different, weak, and sick or in any other kind of need.

As "The Dragon of Greenland" together with the rest of the fleet drifted down the mighty river Thorhilde awakened and asked if she could see Baard the priest. He came and sat next to her and Thorhilde asked that he should give her the Holy Communion for the last time." Regretfully I did not see to that it was done for the dying young woman. Please forgive me my Lord!"

Only minutes after Baard had administered her Holy Communion she sank back and left this earthly life.

The fleet anchored and Thorhilde was dressed and put on display so that everyone could take a last farewell with her. Many cried openly, even hardened men unashamed.

The fleet stayed anchored overnight and they mourned her and Baard gave a sermon of compassion for her were he praised her for everything that she had done for them all. He didn't know all the details from her life but those that did, were asked to come forward and relay their knowledge to them all. Everything was done in a most passionate, solemn and respectful way in a true honor to a beloved Sovereign. Before the burial itself, they saw to that one of the smaller ships would bring the Shawnee scout back home again.

"The Dragon of Greenland" was now anchored in the correct position, in midstream Mississippi River where it met with the Ohio River. The ship was filled with firewood and Thorhilde was laid flat on a built up high deck where they all could see her.

The order to light the fire was given by the captain of her guards. They had been watching over her dead body until now.

Flames were now increasing in power and are soon engulfing the dead body. The settlers are watching this historic event in solemn awe, and are paying their tribute to a great sovereign.

Thorhilde the Viking Queen has gone to her forefathers.